All in Reading

Book One

by Grover K . H . Yu . Ph.D .

三民書局

網路書店位址　http : // www. sanmin. com. tw

©　All in Reading　Ⅰ

編著者　余光雄
發行人　劉振強
著作財
產權人　三民書局股份有限公司
　　　　臺北市復興北路三八六號
發行所　三民書局股份有限公司
　　　　地址／臺北市復興北路三八六號
　　　　電話／二五○○六六○○
　　　　郵撥／○○○九九八——五號
印刷所　三民書局股份有限公司
門市部　復北店／臺北市復興北路三八六號
　　　　重南店／臺北市重慶南路一段六十一號
初版一刷　中華民國八十九年九月
初版三刷　中華民國九十一年八月
編　號　S 80360
行政院新聞局登記證局版臺業字第○二○○號

ISBN　957-14-3285-□　（平裝）

序

　　「閱讀」在學習外（英）語的過程中佔極重要的角色。「閱讀」可說是最方便、最直接且最常用的英語學習途徑。因此，閱讀教材的好壞會直接影響到學習效果。坊間雖然有很多進口的英文教材，但由於不是針對技術學院學生及高職或綜合高中的學生編寫，以至於唸英文變成一種痛苦與折磨，教師在實際教學時也有不便之處。尤其在固定的進度壓力下，授課時數又有限，師生覺得學習英文是萬分的辛苦。

　　《全方位英文閱讀 (All in Reading)》這本英文讀本是在考慮上述諸問題的各層面，以及要幫助師生在課堂內能夠培養聽、說、讀、寫四種技能的均衡發展的需求下而編撰的。這本英文讀本的特色就是它照顧了聽、說、讀、寫四種技能的均衡發展。學生既不必為聽力訓練多帶一本課本，也不必為英文寫作多帶一本課本，因為本讀本就含有這一類的學習材料。這也就是本書取名「全方位英文」的原因。

　　筆者編撰此書時，時時刻刻想到老師要如何教，學生要如何學的問題，所以本英文讀本是以課堂教學為導向、以輕鬆有趣為方針、以生活化為原則，相信定能為學習者帶來事半功倍的效益。其中若有疏漏之處，祈請方家不吝指教。

余光雄　謹識
西元 2000 年六月
於 NKNU

All in Reading (I)
全方位英文閱讀（I）

Unit One

Body Painting

 Pre-reading Activities

Recognize New Words

Learn the Chinese definition of each bold-faced word in the following before you read the text.

1. **decorate** their bodies   裝飾
2. decorate with **designs** (*n.*)   圖像；設計
3. be colored with **dye**   染料
4. be **reflected** in the patterns   反映

5. **warriors** on the battle	戰士
6. **concentrate** on their faces	聚集；集中
7. with red **stripes**	條紋
8. look **fierce and aggressive**	恐怖且具攻擊力
9. be used for **occasions**	場合
10. **the aboriginal**	原住民
11. **permanent** form	永久的
12. the **social status**	社會地位
13. an **individual**	個人
14. decorate their bodies with **tattoos**	刺青
15. **chief**	酋長

Brainstorming Questions

Discuss the following questions with your group members.

1. Some people have certain types of permanent designs painted on their bodies. What are they called? Look up the word "tattoo" in an encyclopedia.

2. In your society, what's the social significance of tattoos?

3. Do you like body painting? Why or why not?

4. How closely is body painting related to culture?

5. Briefly talk about the history of body painting. Refer it to an encyclopedia.

6. Show some pictures or photographs of body painting. Tell the meaning of the painting.

Read the Text

In many cultures, people decorate their bodies with pictures
and designs. Sometimes, the human body is painted or colored
with dye, which can be washed off later. Other forms of body
decoration, such as tattoos, are permanent and stay with the
wearer for life. Very often, people decorate their bodies for a 5
particular purpose, which is reflected in the types of patterns that
they use.

The native people of North America made general use of
body painting. When warriors prepared for battle, they would
paint themselves with bold designs. They concentrated on their 10
faces which were decorated with red stripes, black masks or
white circles around the eyes. These designs made the warrior
look fierce and aggressive. Other peoples also used war-paint.
When the Romans invaded Britain, they found that the ancient
Britons painted themselves with blue paint called woad before 15
going into battle.

Body painting can be used for occasions other than battles.
The Aboriginal of Australia often decorate their bodies with bold
white markings for a corroboree. A corroboree is a special
meeting at which men dance and sing. 20

The Maoris of New Zealand decorated their bodies with
tattooing. This permanent form of body decoration indicated the
social status of an individual. The more important a person was,
the more tattoos they had. Some chiefs and kings had their faces
covered entirely by tattoos. 25

Developing Reading Skills

Use the contextual clues to guess the meaning of a new word.

When you read the text, you find the following underlined words new to you. You don't have to look them up immediately. Instead, you can figure out their meanings from the sentences (contexts) in which they appear.

1. A corroboree is a special meeting at which men dance and sing.

   According to this context, **corroboree** means _____.

2. Other peoples also used war-paint. They found that the ancient Britons painted themselves with blue paint called woad.

   According to the context, **woad** means _____.

3. Other forms of body decoration, such as tattoos, are permanent.

   According to the context, **tattoos** means _____.

Reading Comprehension Check

According to the text you read, answer the following questions.

(   ) 1. What is the main theme of this article?

      (A) People like to decorate their bodies.

      (B) The Aboriginal of Australia like to have body painting.

      (C) Body painting is a special kind of art.

      (D) Body painting is very cultural.

(   ) 2. How many kinds of face painting are used by the native people of North America?

      (A) One　(B) Two　(C) Three　(D) More than three

(   ) 3. Which of the following is true about tattoos?

      (A) The lower the culture is, the more popular tattoos are.

      (B) Civilized people don't like to have tattoos.

      (C) The North American natives gave up having their tattoos.

(D) Among the Maoris, tattoos are symbols of social status.

(   ) 4. What did the ancient Britons paint their bodies with?

    (A) A kind of blue paint called woad.

    (B) Something which is not called woad.

    (C) Stripes with oil paint.

    (D) White paints mixed with black stripes.

(   ) 5. Which of the following statements is NOT true?

    (A) In many cultures people don't like to decorate their bodies with designs.

    (B) Tattoos are a permanent form of body painting.

    (C) The ancient warriors of the North American natives painted their faces to look fierce.

    (D) Chiefs or kings of the Maoris had tattoos on their faces to show social status.

(   ) 6. In which of the following cultures, do people use body decoration as an indication of the social status of an individual?

    (A) The Maoris of New Zealand

    (B) The Aboriginal of Australia

    (C) The native people of North America

    (D) The author didn't give examples.

(   ) 7. From this text, what will you predict the writer's attitude toward tattoos?

    (A) The writer is scared to see them.

    (B) The writer enjoys seeing them.

    (C) The writer likes the ancient types of body painting.

    (D) The writer doesn't indicate his/her particular preference.

(   ) 8. How do people decorate their bodies?

    (A) They decorate their bodies with animals.

(B) They decorate their bodies with various types of dyes.

(C) They decorate their bodies with pictures and designs.

(D) They decorate with stripes, masks and circles around their eyes.

( ) 9. What kind of problem do tattoo-wearers have?

(A) They are not socially respected.

(B) They are not socially respectable.

(C) They can't wash them off when they do not want them.

(D) They have to find doctors to do tattooing for them.

( ) 10. What's the writer's attitude toward body painting?

(A) He/She strongly recommends that young people should go for it.

(B) He/She strongly fights against body painting.

(C) He/She shows neither his preference nor his dislike.

(D) He/She encourages people to experience this type of painting art.

Developing Linguistic Ability

Vocabulary Recognition

Match the words in the left column with the expressions that have similar meaning in the right column.

_____ 1. decorate   (A) make something beautiful by adding ornaments to it

_____ 2. design   (B) a drawing from which something is made

_____ 3. wash off   (C) be removed by water

_____ 4. permanent   (D) ever-lasting

_____ 5. reflect   (E) express (*v.*)

_____ 6. warrior   (F) people who fight in a battle

_____ 7. battle   (G) a fight on the field

_____ 8. bold   (I) daring; brave

_____ 9. concentrate   (J) focus on

_____ 10. stripe   (K) a band of color

_____ 11. fierce   (L) angry and terrible

_____ 12. aggressive   (M) apt to attack

_____ 13. invade   (N) enter with armed force

_____ 14. aboriginal   (O) a native inhabitant

_____ 15. chief   (P) a ruler or leader

Words in Use

Select the best word to fill in the blank.

(   ) 1. His chest was covered with _____.

    (A) tattoos   (B) reflections   (C) aboriginals   (D) individuals

(   ) 2. Their whole life was a constant _____ against poverty.

    (A) warrior   (B) battle   (C) design   (D) status

(   ) 3. It's not easy for a newly graduate to find a(n) _____ employment.

    (A) decorated   (B) aboriginal   (C) permanent   (D) aggressive

(   ) 4. He looked at his face _____ in the mirror.

    (A) decorated   (B) reflected   (C) masked   (D) indicated

(   ) 5. A(n) _____ nation always tries to invade other nations.

    (A) inventive   (B) particular   (C) aggressive   (D) permanent

(   ) 6. Ms. Wang went to the hair saloon to get a hair _____.

    (A) permanent   (B) chief   (C) decoration   (D) design

(   ) 7. Communist China has been trying to _____ Taiwan since 1950's.

    (A) reflect   (B) circle   (C) cover   (D) invade

(   ) 8. Each _____ is responsible for his own life goals.

    (A) design   (B) aggression   (C) circle   (D) individual

(   ) 9. In a particular _____ some awkward expressions should not be used.

(A) tattoo　(B) occasion　(C) battle　(D) invasion

(　) 10. Tigers and lions are ＿＿＿＿＿＿ animals.

(A) aboriginal　(B) permanent　(C) fierce　(D) individual

Phrases in Use

Fill in one proper preposition in the blank.

1. The house was decorated ＿＿＿＿＿＿ seasonable flowers.

2. We dyed the clothes ＿＿＿＿＿＿ blue dye.

3. The marks on your arms can be washed ＿＿＿＿＿＿.

4. The tattoo ＿＿＿＿＿＿ the man's arm looks so scary.

5. She is looking ＿＿＿＿＿＿ a permanent employment.

6. The tattoo will stay ＿＿＿＿＿＿ you forever.

7. He concentrates ＿＿＿＿＿＿ studying for the examination.

8. The Indians often paint their face ＿＿＿＿＿＿ red stripes.

9. He draws a circle ＿＿＿＿＿＿ a pencil.

10. His wife is so aggressive that John is afraid ＿＿＿＿＿＿ her.

11. This is not an occasion ＿＿＿＿＿＿ laughter.

12. There are some markings ＿＿＿＿＿＿ the wall.

13. The arrow indicates the way ＿＿＿＿＿＿ the station.

14. Individual freedom is very important ＿＿＿＿＿＿ democratic countries.

15. He is the chief ＿＿＿＿＿＿ the baseball team.

Vocabulary Development

Give a semantically opposite word for each of the following.

＿＿＿＿ 1. uncover　　(A) warrior

＿＿＿＿ 2. dirty　　(B) aggressive

_____ 3. defend   (C) cover

_____ 4. alien   (D) wash off

_____ 5. servant   (E) king

_____ 6. coward   (F) individual

_____ 7. distract   (G) mask

_____ 8. reveal   (H) attack

_____ 9. general   (I) native

_____10. peaceful   (J) concentrate

Review the text through Cloze Exercise

According to the text you read, select one word for each blank to make a complete and meaningful text. If necessary, make proper changes. Each word should be used only once.

individual	cultures	tattoos	permanent	indicate	dye
aggressive	reflect	decorate	invade	designs	concentrate
warrior	battle	mask	occasion		

In many _____, people decorate their bodies with pictures and _____. Sometimes, the human body is painted or colored with _____, which can be washed off later. Other forms of body decoration, such as _____, are _____ and stay with the wearer for life. Very often, people _____ their bodies for a particular purpose, which is _____ in the types of patterns that they use.

The native people of North America made general use of body painting. When _____ prepared for battle, they would paint themselves with bold designs. They _____ on their faces which were decorated with red stripes, black _____ or white circles around the eyes. These designs made the warrior look fierce and _____. Other peoples also used war-paint. When the Romans

_____ Britain, they found that the ancient Britons painted themselves with blue paint called woad before going into _____.

Body painting can be used for _____ other than battles. The Aboriginal of Australia often decorate their bodies with bold white markings for a corroboree. A corroboree is a special meeting at which men dance and sing.

The Maoris of New Zealand decorated their bodies with tattooing. This permanent form of body decoration _____ the social status of an _____. The more important a person was, the more tattoos they had. Some chiefs and kings had their faces covered entirely by tattoos.

 Speaking Activities

Group Discussion

With your group members discuss the following questions, and then report your answers to the class.

1. What are your group's opinions about having tattoos? Talk about their social significance or artistic value.

2. How and when did the native people of North America paint their faces?

3. What are the possible reasons for warriors to paint their faces to look aggressive?

4. If we treat tattoos as a kind of body painting art, would you like to have some tattoos on your body? Why or why not?

Dialogue Practice

Invite a partner to do the pair work.

T: How much do you know about body painting?

S: Not much. As far as I know, tattooing is one of them.

T: Tattoos are a permanent form of body painting. They stay with the wearer.

S: Do you know how people do tattooing?

T: People decorate the body with a special kind of dye. At the beginning, the person should choose his or her own design and pattern. After that, the design is colored with various kinds of colors.

S: I heard ancient people in some old cultures painted their bodies. Do they do body painting for fun?

T: No. For example, warriors decorated their bodies for a particular purpose. They wanted to look fierce and aggressive.

S: How could they look fierce and aggressive?

T: They painted their faces with scaring colors and designs.

S: In addition to battles, are there any other occasions in which body painting is encouraged?

T: Yes. The Aboriginal of Australia decorate their bodies with bold white markings for a corroboree which is a special meeting for men's dancing and singing.

S: How about in other cultures or countries?

T: Another example is in New Zealand. The Maoris of New Zealand used different kinds of tattoos to indicate their social status.

S: Thank you so much for telling me something about body painting.

 Listening Activities

Listening Comprehension

If the sentence you hear on the tape means the same as the sentence you read in your book, put "S" in the blank; or, put "D" in the blank.

_____ 1. In many cultures, people decorate their bodies with pictures and designs.

_____ 2. Sometimes, the human body is painted or colored with dye, which can not be washed off later.

_____ 3. Tattoos are a permanent form of body decoration and can not be washed off.

_____ 4. The Maoris of New Zealand decorated their bodies to indicate their social status of an individual.

_____ 5. When the warriors of North America prepared for a battle, they painted their faces with bold designs.

Sentence Memory Practice

If the two sentences on the tape you hear mean the same, put "S" in the blank; if not, put "D" in the blank.

1. _____   2. _____   3. _____   4. _____   5. _____

Conversation Comprehension Practice

Listen to the dialogue on the tape carefully. Then answer all the questions at the end.

True or False: According to what you hear on the tape, put "T" before a true statement, and put "F" before a false statement.

_____ 1. The female speaker doesn't like her friends to have tattoos on their bodies.

_____ 2. Tattoo stickers can be washed off, while real tattoos are permanent.

_____ 3. Many young people think having tattoos is a kind of fashion.

_____ 4. Young people think the tattoos on their body can help them look cool.

_____ 5. The male speaker doesn't think that tattoo stickers may attract young people.

_____ 6. The female speaker warns that young people should find out their parents' attitude toward having tattoos on their body.

Writing Activities

Grammar Practice

Part A: Give the correct form of the verb given in the parenthesis for each blank.

1. The warriors _____ (paint) their bodies with dye.

2. Tattoos can't be _____ (wash) off later on.

3. They _____ (decorate) their faces with red stripes, black masks or white circles around the eyes.

4. Body painting can be _____ (use) for other occasions than battles.

5. We may see ourselves _____ (reflect) in the clear water.

Part B: Select a proper preposition for each blank.

_____ 1. _____ many cultures, people decorate their bodies with pictures and designs.

    (A) With   (B) In   (C) At   (D) From

_____ 2. When warriors prepared _____ battle, they would paint themselves with bold designs.

    (A) for   (B) under   (C) of   (D) in

_____ 3. They concentrated _____ their faces which were decorated with red stripes, black masks or white circles around the eyes.

    (A) at (B) on (C) in (D) with

_____ 4. The Maoris of New Zealand decorated their bodies _____ tattooing.

    (A) in (B) of (C) with (D) on

_____ 5. A corroboree is a special meeting _____ which men dance and sing.

    (A) for (B) at (C) on (D) in

Translation

Translate the Chinese portion into English so as to make a complete and grammatical English text.

> Body painting _____（像刺青）could be permanent, and it also can be done _____（用染色）which can be _____ _____（稍後洗掉）.
>
> In Taiwan, among the aboriginal peoples tattoos _____ （表示個人的社經地位）. Modern young people like to have tattoos because they think tattoos can help _____（吸引別人注意）and _____ _____（看起來很酷）. Using tattoo stickers _____（已經 成為一種時尚）.

Structure Practice I

Using an adjective clause to combine two sentences.

Example 1:

1a. You can have the tattoo.

1b. You can't wash it off.

→ *You can have the tattoo **which** can't be washed off.*

Example 2:

2a. Young people like to go to the party.

2b. At the party they can sing and dance.

→ *Young people like to go to the party **at which** they can sing and dance.*

3a. A corroboree is a special party.

3b. At the party men and women can dance and sing.

→ A corroboree is _____

4a. The bird perches on the nest.

4b. On the nest it hatches.

→ The bird perches _____

5a. The witch hid in the house.

5b. In the house she prepared many sweets for children.

→ The witch hid _____

6a. You need to look for the bag.

6b. From the bag you can pick up colorful balls.

→ _____

7a. She bought the newest edition of this dictionary.

7b. For this dictionary she paid about two hundred dollars.

→ _____

Structure Practice II

Follow the example structure to translate each Chinese sentence into English.

Pattern: The + 比較級 + NP + VP, the + 比較級 + NP + VP.

Example: *The more* important a person was, *the more* tattoos they had.

1. 天氣越冷，穿越多衣服。

    The colder _____, the more _____.

2. 車子越大耗油越多。

    The bigger _____, the more _____.

3. 人越有錢越有煩惱。

    The _____, the _____.

Unit Two

Good Luck, Bad Luck

 Pre-reading Activities

Recognize New Words

Learn the Chinese definition of each bold-faced word in the following before you read the text.

1. wear a **bracelet**	手鐲	
2. **be supposed to be**	被認為	
3. a **shell**	貝殼	
4. **keep away**	驅逐	

5. **evil spirits**	惡魔
6. many **beliefs**	信仰
7. **a jar of pennies**	一甕之一分錢的銅板
8. in the **bride**'s shoe	新娘
9. at a **wedding**	婚禮
10. a happy **marriage**	婚姻
11. a **wallet**	男用皮夾
12. a **purse**	女用皮夾
13. make **jangling** noises	叮噹響聲

Brainstorming Questions

Discuss the following questions with your group members.

1. What's the main difference between a belief and a superstition?

2. How many kinds of superstitions can you find in your culture?

3. How does a superstition affect a person's life? Give examples.

4. Is superstition harmful to people?

5. Among Chinese, many believe Feng-shui（風水）. What do you think of it?

Read the Text

Will you have good luck if you carry a silver dollar? Many people believe that carrying a certain coin can bring good luck. Sometimes women wear a coin on a bracelet for luck.

A coin with a hole in it is supposed to be especially lucky in some countries. This idea got started long ago, before coins were used. People believed that a shell or a stone with a hole in it could keep away evil spirits. Coins with a hole would do the same.

5

There are many other beliefs about how money can bring good luck. Here are a few examples. If you find a coin, you will find even more coins. A jar of pennies in the kitchen will bring   10 good luck. A coin in the bride's shoe at a wedding will lead to a happy marriage. If you give a wallet or a purse as a present, put a coin inside. Then the new owner will never be without money.

There are also stories about how money may bring bad luck. One story says that it is unlucky to dream about money. Another   15 story warns about what may happen when you carry coins in a pocket. Shaking the coins and making jangling noises will bring bad luck in love.

20

Reading Comprehension Check

According to the text you read, if the statement is true, put "T" in the blank; if not, put "F" in the blank.

( )   1. Carrying a gold coin will bring people good luck and money.

( )   2. In some countries, people believe that coins are tokens of good luck.

( )   3. Superstition is as old as the use of coins.

( )   4. If you find a coin on the road, the coin will bring you more coins. So, when you are walking, you should look for coins on the roads.

( )   5. It is superstitious to put coins in a wallet which is used as a present.

( )   6. If you dream of coins, the coins will bring you more money. It is true in all cultures.

( )   7. Carrying coins in your pockets may always bring you good luck.

(   )   8. It is believed that young couple in love should not shake the coins in their pockets and make jangling noises.

(   )   9. This article is mainly dealing with superstitions in most cultures.

(   ) 10. The writer of this text did not show his attitude toward superstition.

Developing Linguistic Ability

Vocabulary Recognition

Match the words in the left column with the expressions that have similar meaning in the right column.

_____	1. superstition	(A) a noise made by shaking coins
_____	2. wedding	(B) a ceremony of getting married
_____	3. evil	(C) a small leather bag used by men
_____	4. belief	(D) a container used for keeping things
_____	5. wallet	(E) a small leather bag used by women
_____	6. purse	(F) bad or unlucky
_____	7. jangle	(G) a false belief
_____	8. jar	(H) faith

Words in Use

Select the best word to fill in the blank in each sentence.

(   ) 1. No one ever saw a ghost. Yet, many people believe that there is a ghost. This is truly a false _____ .

     (A) belief   (B) legend   (C) wedding   (D) wallet

(   ) 2. Do you think Chinese Feng-shui is _____ ?

     (A) lucky   (B) superstitions   (C) legendary   (D) evil

(   ) 3. It is a superstition that coins can _____ evil spirits.

(A) keep away   (B) take care of   (C) deal with   (D) carry away

(   ) 4. The child was given a watch as a _____.

    (A) belief   (B) wedding   (C) present   (D) president

(   ) 5. When you _____ hands with people, hold their hand steadily.

    (A) rake   (B) bake   (C) brake   (D) shake

(   ) 6. People get divorced because they have a broken _____.

    (A) shortage   (B) wedding   (C) marriage   (D) carriage

(   ) 7. Red is often used to _____ people about what may bring about

    danger.

    (A) care   (B) dream   (C) warn   (D) laugh

(   ) 8. Many women wear bracelets with coins _____ good luck.

    (A) for   (B) of   (C) with   (D) from

(   ) 9. The thing that women wear around their wrist is called a _____.

    (A) fashion   (B) collar   (C) ring   (D) bracelet

(   ) 10. Scientists still have no evidence to _____ the existence of evil

    spirits.

    (A) report   (B) indicate   (C) prove   (D) protect

Structure Growth

Select the best answer to fill in the blank.

(   ) 1. Superstition is often related _____ culture and religion.

    (A) to   (B) with   (C) of   (D) for

(   ) 2. Stones or shells would protect them _____ evil spirits.

    (A) for   (B) to   (C) as   (D) from

(   ) 3. People think good luck may accompany _____ a coin with a hole in it.

    (A) to   (B) as   (C) with   (D) for

(   ) 4. _____ addition, there are other superstitions that coins will bring

    good luck.

(A) To   (B) With   (C) As   (D) In

(   ) 5. For instance, _____ that if you find a coin, it will bring you much more coins.

   (A) it says   (B) it is said   (C) people said   (D) men say

(   ) 6. A coin in the bride's shoe at the wedding is believed to lead _____ a happy marriage.

   (A) to   (B) for   (C) forth   (D) up

(   ) 7. _____, if you want to give people presents and choose the wallet or purse at last, remember to put a coin into it.

   (A) That's to say   (B) It's better

   (C) What's more   (D) The other hand

(   ) 8. There will be always money in it; _____, the new owner will never be lack for money.

   (A) what is more   (B) it is said   (C) namely   (D) that was to say

(   ) 9. _____, there are also numerous stories about how the money comes with bad luck.

   (A) In some way   (B) In another words

   (C) Certainly   (D) On the other hand

(   ) 10. It is a bad thing to dream _____ money because this kind of dreams will bring people bad luck.

   (A) to   (B) of   (C) in   (D) at

(   ) 11. _____ you _____ good luck because you own a silver coin?

   (A) Do...never get   (B) Did...never wish

   (C) Have...ever had   (D) Will...ever have

(   ) 12. Others say that people _____ better not hold the coins or money when they are in the pocket.

   (A) have   (B) had   (C) would   (D) will

Speaking Activities

Group Discussion

Form groups of four and discuss the following questions. Then, report your answers to the class.

1. Why do people think good luck may accompany with a coin with a hole in it?

2. According to the text, what may be put in the kitchen to have good luck?

3. According to the text, what should the bride do to wish a happy marriage at the wedding ceremony?

4. Why should we put a coin in the purse or wallet when giving it as a present to others?

5. What kind of superstitions about money is unlucky for love according to the text?

Dialogue Practice

Find a partner to act out the following dialogue.

A: Why do you wear bracelets?

B: To protect myself from evil spirits.

A: To protect yourself from evil spirits? I can't understand that.

B: Haven't you heard that a bracelet can protect you from breaking your arms when falling down to the ground?

A: I know that wearing a helmet can protect me from breaking my head. I've never heard about wearing a bracelet can protect me from breaking my arms.

B: Do you think I am superstitious?

A: If you are not superstitious, what else is?

B: I would rather believe that than break my arms. You idiot!

A: Who's an idiot? Ha-Ha! (Laughing).

Listening Activities

Sentence Comprehension

If the sentence you hear on the tape means the same as the one you read on your book, put "S" in the blank; if not, put "D" in the blank.

_____ 1. There is a superstition that carrying a coin will bring people bad luck.

_____ 2. Wearing a coin on a bracelet is a kind of tokens of good luck.

_____ 3. Putting a coin in the bride's shoe at the wedding ceremony is believed to lead to a happy marriage.

_____ 4. It is said people had better not hold the coins when they are in the pocket.

_____ 5. It is bad to believe that dreaming of money will bring a person bad luck.

Answer Questions

You will hear narrations and some questions on the tape. According to what you hear on the tape, select the best answers to the questions.

(　　) 1. (A) Rings and necklaces   (B) Strings and necklaces

      (C) Pins and bracelets   (D) Rings and bracelets

(　　) 2. (A) Superstition has a long history, especially longer than the history of culture.

      (B) Superstition has long existed, and its history is as long as that of coins.

(C) The history of superstition is longer than that of coins.

(D) The history of superstition is not longer than that of coins.

(　) 3. (A) Before the wedding ceremony　　(B) After the wedding ceremony

(C) At the wedding ceremony　　(D) During the wedding ceremony

(　) 4. (A) We need to discover more legends about coins.

(B) More superstitions about coins can't be found by us.

(C) There are more superstitions of coins to be discovered.

(D) The world has a trend to discover all the superstitions about coins.

(　) 5. (A) Jenny's mother found no other better place to put her pennies.

(B) Jenny's mother thought jars are the best places to save her pennies.

(C) Jenny's mother thought the jars in the kitchen were the safest place to save pennies.

(D) Jenny's mother believed saving pennies in the jar in the kitchen would bring her more pennies.

Writing Activities

Writing Practice

Combine each pair of sentences (a, b) into one.

1a. This is a superstition.

1b. Carrying a coin will bring people good luck.

→ _____

2a. Many women wear bracelets.

2b. The bracelets are decorated with coins.

→ _____

3a. The story is related to the belief.

3b. That carrying coins will bring good luck is the belief.

→ _____

4a. You will have good luck.

4b. You put a jar of pennies in the kitchen.

→ _____

5a. To dream of money is bad.

5b. It is said.

→ _____

Correcting Grammatical Errors

There are several grammatical errors in the following text. Identify them and give corrections in the blanks. (Review the whole sentence.)

1. Did you ever had good luck because of you own a silver coin?

2. There are a superstition that carry a coin will bring people good luck.

3. However, many woman wear bracelets is a token of good luck.

4. This superstition is relating to the belief when things such as stones or shells would protect them from evil souls and spirits.

5. Superstition got started long before, before coins were using.

Answers:

1. _____

2. _____

3. _____

4. _____

5. _____

Unit Three

Language in Clothes

 Pre-reading Activities

Recognize New Words

Learn the Chinese definition of each bold-faced word in the following before you read the text.

1. use **make-up**   化粧品
2. particular **fashions**   時尚
3. a very **obvious** form   明顯的
4. the name of an **organization**   組織；機構

5. the name of a **product**   產品

6. wear **specific** clothes   特別的

7. special **occasions**   場合

8. more **elaborate**   精緻的

9. a **suit with tails**   燕尾服

10. wear an **outfit**   外套

11. with **embroidered** dragons   刺繡的

12. attend **funerals**   喪禮

13. an **armband**   臂章

14. a **sorrowful** mood   哀傷的

Brainstorming Questions

Discuss the following questions with your group members.

1. What's the cultural significance of clothes?

2. What kind of characteristics can we identify from the clothes people wear?

3. Why do women follow clothes fashions more faithfully than men?

4. What characteristics can we find in the clothes Chinese people wear?

5. Show a picture of particular clothes you like.

Read the Text

Although body painting is now unusual in many cultures, most people still decorate their bodies in some ways—using make-up, jewelry and clothes. Clothes in particular are a kind of body language. People often wear particular styles and fashions in order to give out a message or to say what kind of person they are.   5

A T-shirt with a message is a very obvious form of communication in clothing. The T-shirt may carry the name of a pop group, club or organization. This clothing shows the musical taste of the wearers, or tells everyone that they support a 10 particular club. Some people wear a T-shirt with the name of a product as a form of advertising.

Sometimes people wear specific clothes for special occasions. If a woman gets married she may wear an expensive wedding dress which is much longer and more elaborate than 15 her normal clothes. The man being married might wear a top hat and a suit with tails, neither of which he would wear in ordinary life. Different cultures and religions have different traditions about wedding clothes. At Christian weddings, it is usual for the bride to wear white. Hindus and Sikhs 20 often wear very brightly colored clothes. A Chinese bride may wear an outfit decorated with embroidered dragons and phoenixes, 25 which are signs of good luck.

All these special clothes show that the couple consider marriage to be a joyful and special event. When attending funerals, people in many different cultures normally wear dark clothes, sometimes with a black tie or an armband. Black is a 30 sign of a sorrowful mood.

Reading Comprehension Check

According to the text you read, answer the following questions.

(　　) 1. In the following passage, you will read four sentences. Which of the following statements can best describe the textual relationships among them?

(1) A T-shirt with a message is a very obvious form of communication in clothing. (2) The T-shirt may carry the name of a pop group, club or organization. (3) This clothing shows the musical taste of the wearers, or tells everyone that they support a particular club. (4) Some people wear a T-shirt with the name of a product as a form of advertising.

(A) The first sentence is a topic sentence, and the rest are supporting sentences.

(B) The last sentence is a topic sentence, and the rest give supporting ideas.

(C) The second sentence illustrates the first, and the last supports the third.

(D) All these four sentences can be rearranged in any order we like.

(　　) 2. Which of the four given sentences has the similar meaning to the sentence you will read below?

"Although body painting is now unusual in many cultures, most people still decorate their bodies in some way—using make-up, jewelry and clothes."

(A) Most people use make-up, jewelry, etc. as ornaments to decorate their bodies because body painting is now common everywhere.

(B) Body painting is not in fashion in many countries, but lots of people can use cosmetics, jewelry and clothes to decorate their bodies.

(C) Make-up, jewelry, and clothes are ways that people use to decorate their bodies since body painting is not popular in many areas of the world.

(D) In many cultures cosmetics, jewels and clothes are so much in high demands that body painting will soon become popular.

( ) 3. What is the main idea of the third paragraph of the text you read?

(A) People wear specific clothes for special occasions.

(B) Brides wear white dresses for the wedding.

(C) Hindus like to wear brightly colored clothes.

(D) Different kinds of clothes indicate different kinds of lack.

( ) 4. Which of the following has the same meaning as the word "specific" in "Sometimes people wear **specific** clothes for special occasion."?

(A) splendid   (B) expensive   (C) particular   (D) new

( ) 5. Which of the following means the same as "decorated" in "an outfit **decorated** with embroidered dragons..."?

(A) designed   (B) enlarged   (C) produced   (D) adorned

Developing Linguistic Ability

Vocabulary Growth

( ) 1. When attending a _____, people normally wear dark clothes.

(A) wedding   (B) funeral   (C) channel   (D) marriage

( ) 2. Following _____ can be quite expensive.

(A) crowds   (B) ideals   (C) tattoos   (D) fashions

( ) 3. Seeing off a good friend, her eyes are full of _____ tears.

(A) sorrowful   (B) moody   (C) funeral   (D) elaborate

( ) 4. He gave a(n) _____ answer to the question.

(A) elaborate   (B) tailed   (C) occasional   (D) productive

(   )   5. He wore a cap with a(n) ＿＿＿＿＿ ★ mark.

      (A) suitable   (B) jewelry   (C) embroidered   (D) decoration

(   )   6. ＿＿＿＿＿ is a collective noun which does not have a plural form.

      (A) Clothing   (B) Wearing   (C) Fashion   (D) Suit

(   )   7. ETS stands for Educational Testing Services, which is a(n) ＿＿＿＿＿ that takes charge of TOEFL tests.

      (A) permanence   (B) organization   (C) occasion   (D) reference

(   )   8. It is ＿＿＿＿＿ that English has become an international language.

      (A) fashionable   (B) occasional   (C) organizational   (D) obvious

(   )   9. Taiwan makes money by exporting industrial ＿＿＿＿＿.

      (A) clothing   (B) products   (C) suits   (D) tattoos

(   ) 10. How do Taiwanese ＿＿＿＿＿ their houses to celebrate New Year?

      (A) decorate   (B) design   (C) elaborate   (D) participate

Morphology

Some adjectives can be formed from a noun by adding a suffix "-al" or "-able" to the end of the word. Try to form an adjective for each of the following.

1. fashion → ＿＿＿＿＿＿＿

2. music → ＿＿＿＿＿＿＿

3. occasion → ＿＿＿＿＿＿＿

4. norm → ＿＿＿＿＿＿＿

5. culture → ＿＿＿＿＿＿＿

Structural Growth I

Many noun phrases can be modified by a prepositional phrase through which we can expand the structure of a constituent. Try to expand the following phrases by adding a prepositional phrase to the end.

Example:（很多文化裡的）body painting → body painting *in many cultures*

1.（特別的）clothes → clothes _____

2.（帶有訊息的）a T-shirt → a T-shirt _____

3.（穿者的）musical taste → musical taste _____

4.（帶有產品名稱的）T-shirts → T-shirts _____

5.（繡有龍鳳的）an outfit → an outfit _____

Structural Growth II

Many noun phrases can be modified by a present participial phrase (V-ing Phrase) or a past participial phrase (V-ed Phrase). Try to expand the following noun phrases.

Example:（結過婚的男人）the married man → the man *being married*

1.（離婚的女人）the divorced woman → the woman _____

2.（染了鮮艷色彩的衣服）the brightly colored clothes → the clothes _____

3.（煮沸過的水）the boiled water → the water _____

4.（分居的夫婦）the separated couple → the couple _____

5.（已開發國家）the developed country → the country _____

Speaking Activities

Group Discussion

Give answers to each of the following questions. Report your answers to the class. You may do this with your group members.

1. Discuss why body painting is still **unusual** in many cultures.

2. Discuss why a Chinese bride may wear **an outfit** decorated with embroidered dragons and phoenixes. What are their cultural significance?

3. Explain why a T-shirt with a message is a very obvious form of communication in clothing.

Role Play

Find a partner to act out the following dialogue. You play the part A.

A: (Praise your friend on the dress she wears today.)

B: (Thanks for the compliment.)

A: (Ask about the style of the dress.)

B: (Tell and describe the dress you wear.)

A: (Ask if there are any special reasons to wear this dress today.)

B: (Answer A's questions.)

A: (Ask if B wears new clothes on Chinese New Year's Day. And why.)

B: (Answer A's questions.)

 *Listening Activities*

Sentence Dictation

Listen to each sentence on the tape, and fill in one missing word in each blank.

1. Clothes in particular are a kind of body _____.

2. A T-shirt with a message is a very _____ form of communication in clothing.

3. People wear particular fashions in order to give out a _____.

4. A wedding dress is more _____ than normal clothes.

5. When attending _____, people wear dark clothes to show a sorrowful mood.

6. Some wear T-shirts with the name of a product as a form of _____ .

7. Different _____ have different traditions about wedding clothes.

8. A T-shirt may carry the name of an _____ .

9. Many clothing show the particular _____ of the wearers.

10. An outfit decorated with _____ dragons and phoenixes is unusual.

Sentence Comprehension

If the two sentences on the tape you hear mean the same, put "S" in the blank; if not, put "D" in the blank.

1. _____   2. _____   3. _____   4. _____   5. _____

Writing Activities

Identify Grammatical Errors

There are a few grammatical errors in the following passage. Underline the errors, and write the correct answers in the blanks given below the passage.

> All these special clothes shows that the couples consider marriage is a joy and special event. When attend funerals, people in many different culture normal wear dark clothes, sometime with a black tie or armband. Black is a sign of a sorrow mood.

Answers:

1. *shows → show*   2. _____   3. _____

4. _____   5. _____   6. _____

7. _____   8. _____   9. _____

10. _____

Sentence Completion

Based on the content of the text you read, try to complete each of the following.
Try to create your own sentences.

1. A Chinese bride may wear an outfit _____ dragons and

   phoenixes, which are _____.

2. A T-shirt which _____ a message is an _____

   of communication in _____.

3. Some people wear clothes with _____ as a form of

   _____.

4. People wear particular styles in order to _____.

5. Chinese people consider wedding to be _____ and should

   wear _____.

Using Connectives in the Text

Fill in one proper word (connectives) to make the passage coherent.

_____1_____ body painting is now unusual in many cultures, most people still decorate their bodies in some ways _____2_____ using make-up, jewelry and clothes. Clothes in particular are a kind of body language. People often wear clothes _____3_____ have particular styles and fashions in order to give out a message _____4_____ tells people what kind of person the wearers are.

For example, a T-shirt _____5_____ has a message is a very obvious form of communication in clothing. The T-shirt _____6_____ carries the name of a club or organization is communicating a message through _____7_____ we can tell what the wearer is. _____8_____, this type of clothing shows certain kind of taste of the wearers, or tells everyone _____9_____ they support a particular club. _____10_____, wearing clothes is not simply putting on garments. We are what we wear.

Answers:

1. _____   2. _____   3. _____   4. _____

5. _____   6. _____   7. _____   8. _____

9. _____   10. _____

Paragraph Writing

In the following given situation, write a paragraph of 80 words in length to tell your opinions about wearing clothes.

Do you think clothes can really convey（傳達）what the wearer thinks, or do you think clothes are merely something that covers your body and keeps you warm?

_____

_____

_____

_____

_____

_____

_____

_____

_____

_____

Translation

Translate each of the following Chinese into English.

1. 中國新娘可能會穿繡有龍鳳圖樣的服裝。這些刺繡是吉祥的象徵。

_____

_____

2. 縱使人體彩繪目前在許多文化中仍不普遍，大多數人仍以其他方法裝飾自己；例
   如：化粧、珠寶跟衣服。

   _____

   _____

Unit Four

Animal Communication

 Pre-reading Activities

Learn the Chinese definition of each bold-faced word in the following before you read the text.

1. **mating rituals**	交配歷程
2. the same **species**	物種
3. make special **signals**	信號
4. return to the **hive**	蜂巢

5. **wriggle** its body   蠕動

6. facial **expressions**   表情

7. **pout** as a sign of greeting   噘嘴

8. **jut out** their jaws   伸出

Brainstorming Questions

With your group members discuss the following questions.

1. How do animals communicate with each other?

2. What are the differences between human communication and animal communication? Find the answer in a linguistic book.

3. How do you communicate with your pet?

4. Why can't people teach animals to use human language?

Read the Text

Although body language is an important part of animal mating rituals, it is a vital means of communication in many other situations too. Many animals have greeting rituals. When different members of the same species meet in the wild, they may be uncertain whether they are facing an enemy or a friend.   5 So they go through careful greeting rituals to make sure that the other animal does not intend to attack.

Other animals make special signals to warn the members of their species if there is danger nearby. One kind of deer in North America has a white tail. When it is frightened, it runs away with   10 its white tail held upright in the air. The other deer see this warning sign and know to run away too.

Honey bees also use body signals to pass on information. They spend the summer collecting pollen and nectar from flowers to make honey. During the winter, this honey will provide   15 them with food. If a bee finds a large group of flowers, it returns to the hive. There it "dances," flying around in a figure of eight, wriggling and shaking its body as it does so. When the other bees see these movements, they learn where the flowers are and fly out to harvest the pollen.   20

Like humans, animals also express their moods and feelings through facial expressions. Chimpanzees open their mouths wide and show their teeth when they are frightened or excited. They often pout as   25 a sign of greeting and press their lips together and jut out their jaws when they want to look threatening.

Comprehension Check through Cloze Test

According to the text you just read, select one proper word for each blank.

Except mating rituals, body language is a(n) ____1____ part in animal communication in other situations. Animals like ____2____ can also use some signals to express some specific meanings, such as greeting, warning, conveyance of information, and feelings. Let's ____3____ some animal behaviors for example. Some animals would make ____4____ greeting when they are uncertain ____5____ the same species are friends or enemies. In North America, one kind of deer would raise its white tail ____6____ the air to warn other deer to run

_____7_____ when it _____8_____ the danger nearby. When honey bees find a group of flowers, they would go back to their _____9_____ and "dance" in a figure of eight, _____10_____ their bodies, to tell other bees where the pollen and nectar are.

_____11_____ chimpanzees? They are the animals that resemble human beings more than _____12_____ on earth. Chimpanzees _____13_____ human beings also have some facial expressions to express their feelings, _____14_____ pouting as a greeting, pressing their lips together and _____15_____ out their jaws for threat.

(   ) 1. (A) special   (B) important   (C) small   (D) useful

(   ) 2. (A) plants   (B) computers   (C) human beings   (D) music

(   ) 3. (A) take   (B) make   (C) use   (D) do

(   ) 4. (A) enthusiastic   (B) careful   (C) hostile   (D) indifferent

(   ) 5. (A) that   (B) which   (C) as   (D) whether

(   ) 6. (A) in   (B) on   (C) above   (D) around

(   ) 7. (A) across   (B) after   (C) down   (D) away

(   ) 8. (A) sees   (B) looks   (C) touches   (D) smells

(   ) 9. (A) houses   (B) hives   (C) cages   (D) nests

(   ) 10. (A) wriggle and shake   (B) moving and dancing

         (C) wriggling and shaking   (D) wriggled and shaken

(   ) 11. (A) How about   (B) What if   (C) How is   (D) What for

(   ) 12. (A) any other   (B) any others   (C) any ones   (D) any other ones

(   ) 13. (A) as   (B) like   (C) such as   (D) so as

(   ) 14. (A) example of   (B) such that   (C) such as   (D) like as

(   ) 15. (A) raising   (B) wriggling   (C) shaking   (D) jutting

Reading for the Detail

According to the text, select the best answer to the questions.

(   ) 1. What do animals use body language for?

(A) For mating and expressing specific information and feelings.

(B) For showing gestures and sounds so as to communicate.

(C) For showing beautiful appearances to attract animals of other sexes.

(D) For communicating with other species and their peers.

( ) 2. When would deer in North America raise their white tails?

(A) It is a mating ritual.

(B) To guide the deer behind them.

(C) To show off their beautiful tails.

(D) To warn other deer of the danger nearby.

( ) 3. How do honey bees tell others where the food is?

(A) They tell others with their buzzing sounds.

(B) They fly around in a figure of eight.

(C) They wave their wings to tell others to follow them.

(D) They tell other bees directly where the food is.

( ) 4. Which animals use facial expressions like human beings do ?

(A) Chimpanzees   (B) American deer   (C) Monkeys   (D) Dogs

( ) 5. What would chimpanzees do when they want to look threatening?

(A) They roar threateningly.

(B) They wave their strong fists.

(C) They jut out their jaws.

(D) They throw rocks toward enemies.

Developing Linguistic Ability

Vocabulary Development

Learn the definitions of the new words. Match the words in Group A with the definitions in Group B.

Group A	Group B
_____ 1. excited	(A) routine work
_____ 2. communication	(B) a sign or symbol
_____ 3. ritual	(C) offend
_____ 4. attack	(D) stimulated
_____ 5. signal	(E) ways to convey messages
_____ 6. threatening	(F) systems for transportation
	(G) warning and frightening

Group A	Group B
_____ 7. upright	(H) a kind of powder from flowers
_____ 8. collect	(I) accumulate; put together
_____ 9. nectar	(J) shape
_____ 10. hive	(K) gently move like worms
_____ 11. figure	(L) a nest for bees
_____ 12. wriggle	(M) a kind of fruit
_____ 13. pollen	(N) in vertical position
_____ 14. pout	(O) a type of pollen
_____ 15. frightened	(P) scared, or terrified
	(Q) pull out lips to show anger

Synonyms

Give a semantically similar word for each of the following.

_____ 1. threatening	(A) nest
_____ 2. hive	(B) sign
_____ 3. attack	(C) offend
_____ 4. signal	(D) shape

_____ 5. figure

(E) defend

(F) warning and frightening

Antonyms

Match one antonym for each of the following in the left column.

_____ 1. vital   (A) tame

_____ 2. wild   (B) useless, trivial

_____ 3. uncertain   (C) defend

_____ 4. attack   (D) sure

_____ 5. danger   (E) close

_____ 6. nearby   (F) far

                       (G) safety

Vocabulary in Use

Select the best word to fill in the blank in each of the following.

( ) 1. The issues presented at the meeting are of _____ importance.

   (A) complicated   (B) ritual   (C) virtual   (D) vital

( ) 2. _____ is the major function of language.

   (A) Intervention   (B) Communication

   (C) Conversation   (D) Interpretation

( ) 3. It is a Chinese _____ to worship their ancestors on the New Year's Day.

   (A) ritual   (B) recital   (C) respect   (D) rural

( ) 4. Our army _____ the enemy's camp during the night.

   (A) attacked   (B) arrested   (C) dispatched   (D) disclosed

( ) 5. A red light is a _____ usually used to signify a dangerous situation.

   (A) lamp   (B) significance   (C) signal   (D) lantern

(   ) 6. Please help me to adjust the photocopy machine to a(n) _____ position.

     (A) prospective   (B) dimensional   (C) applicable   (D) upright

(   ) 7. There is no way of knowing the number of bees in their _____.

     (A) dwelling   (B) residence   (C) home   (D) hive

(   ) 8. The hungry dog ran away, _____ its tail. It looked so cute.

     (A) waving   (B) barking   (C) wriggling   (D) biting

(   ) 9. Bees busily collect _____ from flowers in summer.

     (A) pollution   (B) population   (C) potential   (D) pollen

(   ) 10. Chimpanzees _____ when they show friendly greeting.

     (A) spout   (B) pout   (C) jut out   (D) strain

(   ) 11. The predicted cold weather seems to be _____.

     (A) treated   (B) threatening   (C) thawed   (D) threading

(   ) 12. The poor country must have _____ many wars.

     (A) gone over   (B) gone through

     (C) passed through   (D) passed over

(   ) 13. Chimpanzees open their mouths wide and show their teeth when they are _____.

     (A) threatened   (B) greeted   (C) patted   (D) frightened

(   ) 14. The teacher asked students to _____ the handouts _____ to the next person.

     (A) give...out   (B) pass...down   (C) pass...on   (D) divide...up

(   ) 15. Animals like human beings show their moods and feelings _____ facial expressions.

     (A) through   (B) by   (C) with   (D) from

Phrase Drill

Select from the list a proper phrase to insert into each sentence. Sometimes, adjustments of word forms are necessary.

| go through | run away | pass on | make sure | jut out |

1. He had _____ lots of hardship before he achieved his success.

2. We can't _____ whether or not the meeting time is at 3 o'clock.

3. The criminal broke the window and _____.

4. The teacher would like us to _____ the homework _____ each individual.

5. When the chimp is angry, he _____ his jaw to look fierce.

 Speaking Activities

Group Work

With your group members discuss the following questions. Then, report your answers to the class.

1. What's the function of animals' greeting rituals? Do they mean the same as those of human beings?

2. How do animals do when they meet other animals but aren't sure they are enemies or friends?

3. What would you think if you saw a deer running with its tail upright in the air?

4. How do bees pass on information? What will they do if they find a large group of flowers?

5. How do chimpanzees express their excitement or fear? And how do they greet each other?

6. How do human beings greet each other? Do these rituals mean the same as those of other animals?

Dialogue Practice

Find a partner to practice the following dialogue.

Work Bee: I've found lots of pollen over there!

King Bee: Where exactly?

Work Bee: The pollen is on the tall red roses over there.

King Bee: How far is it from here? Can you be a little more specific?

Work Bee: It's not too far from here. Watch me. [The bee starts dancing.]

King Bee: Yes, it's not too far from here. In what direction?

Work Bee: Look at my head while I am dancing.

King Bee: Got it. Everybody, listen. Let's follow Work Bee to collect pollen.

 *Listening Activities*

Sentence Comprehension

If the sentence you hear on the tape means the same as the one you read in your textbook, put "S" in the blank; if not, put "D" in the blank.

_____ 1. The greeting rituals between animals and human beings are almost the same.

_____ 2. Animals can use body language to identify whether they are facing friends or enemies.

_____ 3. The reason why animals have to use special body language is to make sure that the other animals won't be attacked.

_____ 4. Bees dance to pass on information.

_____ 5. Bees inform their peers about where to find flowers by means of dancing in a figure of eight.

_____ 6. Like human beings chimpanzees use facial expressions to show their moods and feelings.

_____ 7. While in danger, chimpanzees usually jut out their jaws to look threatening.

Sentence Dictation

Listen to the sentences on the tape carefully, and fill in the missing words in the blanks.

1. Except mating _____, body language plays an important part in animal communication.

2. There are animals that _____ human beings more than any _____ ones.

3. They would make careful _____ when they are _____ whether the same _____ they meet are friends or enemies.

4. They tell their fellow bees where the _____ and _____ are.

5. Like human beings, _____ can make some _____ expressions.

Writing Activities

Sentence Completion

Use your own words to complete each of the following.

1. Like _____（成人一樣）, children have to communicate with _____（手勢）.

2. Because animals _____（不會使用人類語言）, they have to use body language to communicate.

3. Body language is considered _____（重要的溝通工具）in many different countries.

4. Students made noise to make sure that _____（狗被嚇跑了）.

5. The dog ran away with _____（一條長尾巴）held upright in the air.

6. Students signed to tell where _____（盒子藏在何處）.

7. They _____（用臉部表情）as a sign of _____（抗議）.

Reinforcing Structure

Match the structures arranged in 1, 2, 3... order with the structures arranged in the alphabetical order.

_____ 1. I did not know   a. more than any other ones.

_____ 2. The picnic will be cancelled   b. whether he was coming or not.

_____ 3. We went swimming   c. when it smells the danger.

_____ 4. There are chimps that resemble   d. even though it was cold.
          human beings

_____ 5. The deer would raise its tail   e. only if it rains.

_____ 6. Bees use their body language   f. difficulties to finish her work.

_____ 7. Make sure   g. to pass on information.

_____ 8. Mary went through   h. that you come to class on time.

_____ 9. Although it was cold,   i. I went swimming.

_____10. I am going swimming tomorrow   j. whether it is cold or not.

Structure Focus

The phrase "make sure" can be followed by (1) an infinitive phrase or (2) a that-clause. Look at the examples.

Structure One: Make sure + to V + ...

Structure Two: Subj. + make sure + that-clause

Example:

Structure One: *Make sure to close the windows before you leave the room.*

Structure Two: *They can't make sure that they can turn in the work in time.*

Translate each of the following into English.

1. 我們有把握準時到達。

_____

2. 她確保能把房間弄乾淨。

_____

3. 我無法確定每件事完美無缺。

_____

4. 我無法確保她會遵守諾言。

_____

5. 請務必把此訊息傳送給他。

_____

6. 颱風來臨前，務必做好防颱準備。

_____

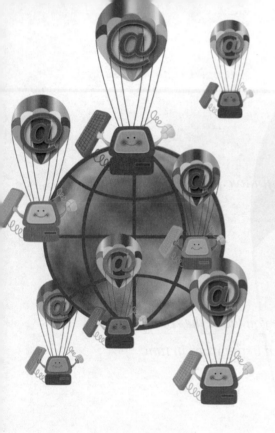

~As you sow, so shall you reap.

Unit Five

Take a Walk

 Pre-reading Activities

Recognize New Words

Learn the Chinese definition of each bold-faced word in the following before you read the text.

    1. run **for exercise** 　　　　　　　　為了運動（此處 run for 不可視為片語）

    2. require no special **equipment** 　　　設備（無複數形）

    3. give the same **benefits** 　　　　　　利益

    4. put more **stress** on your legs 　　　　壓力

5. a steady and **continuous motion**   不停的動作

6. set **goals** for themselves   目標

7. a **definite course** to walk   固定路線

Brainstorming Questions

Discuss the following questions with your group members.

1. Can walking be regarded as one type of exercise? Why or why not?

2. What should one do if one would treat walking as a kind of exercise?

3. Compare jogging with walking. Discuss similarities and differences.

Read the Text

Many people run for sport or exercise. But what if you are not a "born" runner or jogger? You may still want a sport that's inexpensive and easy to do. Why not try walking?

Walking is something that almost any normal, healthy person can do. It requires no special equipment. Walking can   5 give you many of the same benefits as jogging or running; it will just take longer. Jogging and running make your heart and lungs work harder than walking. They also put more stress on your legs and feet than walking does.

The problem with walking as a kind of exercise is that most   10 people don't take it seriously. But there's a big difference between serious walking and the kind of walking that most of us do. Walking, like jogging, should have a steady and continuous motion.

If you're going to get your exercise by walking, you need to   15
have your own walking program. After all, runners and joggers
set goals for themselves. Walkers need goals, too.

Set a definite course to walk. Start by walking about 15–30
minutes a day. Build up your time and distance slowly. Try
increasing your walking speed little by little.   20

If jogging or running is your sport, follow the same advice.
Start off slowly. Spend most of the first few days just walking.
Then start walking and running on the same day. Run or jog a
short distance, then walk for a
while, then run, then walk.   25
Follow that pattern for 15–30
minutes a day. Slowly make
each run longer and each walk
shorter. Later on, you can
increase your distance, speed,   30
and exercise time.

Reading Comprehension Check

According to the text you read, if the statement is true, put "T" in the blank; if not, put "F" in the blank.

(   ) 1. Walking requires special equipment.

(   ) 2. Walking gives your heart and lungs more stress than jogging.

(   ) 3. Most people don't take walking as a kind of exercise seriously.

(   ) 4. Walking has the same benefits as running.

(   ) 5. We should set a definite course to walk.

(   ) 6. Walkers should set goals for themselves.

(   ) 7. Walkers may start by walking about 15–30 minutes a day.

(   ) 8. If we want to treat walking as a kind of exercise, it's better to start off slowly.

(   ) 9. We can start walking and running on the same day.

(   ) 10. We can lose our weight by walking.

Developing Linguistic Ability

Vocabulary Development

Learn the English definition of each of the following words. Match them.

_____ 1. jogging   (A) not jokingly

_____ 2. equipment   (B) parts of your organs

_____ 3. stress (*n.*)   (C) objective

_____ 4. lungs   (D) pressure

_____ 5. seriously   (E) slow running, a kind of exercise

_____ 6. goal   (F) facilities needed for doing something

_____ 7. definite   (G) certain or regulated

Words in Use

Select the best word to fill in the blank.

(   ) 1. The thing that doesn't cost much is usually _____.

       (A) unnecessary   (B) uncertain   (C) inexpensive   (D) indefinite

(   ) 2. To do a science project normally _____ time and energy.

       (A) requires   (B) expects   (C) costs   (D) increases

(   ) 3. A good university should have excellent professors as well as advanced _____.

       (A) equipment   (B) conditions   (C) experts   (D) continuity

(　) 4. Successful people usually have clearly set their _____ for their
careers.

　(A) dreams　　　(B) expectations　(C) stress　　　(D) goals

(　) 5. My teacher often says, "I am _____. I'm not joking." when he really
means it.

　(A) hurt　　　　(B) laughing　　(C) hard　　　　(D) serious

Phrase Drills

Fill in one proper word in each blank.

1. If students don't _____ foreign languages seriously, they will never
_____ them _____.

2. Walking does not _____ as much stress _____ legs and feet as
jogging does.

3. If you want to have a good grade, the homework given by the teacher should
be _____ seriously.

4. Most successful businessmen _____ goals _____ themselves at
their young age.

5. New students should _____ the advice given by seniors so as to improve
grades.

6. If we want to get our exercise _____ walking, we need to have our
_____ walking program.

7. We can _____ _____ our vocabulary knowledge by memorization.

8. Walking should be _____ _____ slowly to avoid sports injuries.

9. As for jogging, you may slowly make each run longer and each walk shorter.
_____ _____, you can join a long distance race.

10. Do they have problems _____ accurate pronunciation?

Pattern Drills

Use the given structures to translate each of the following into English.

Structure One: Why not + Verb (Root) + ...?

Example: *Why not go to the movies?*

Structure Two: NP + spend + NP [time (in) or money (on)] + V-ing

Example: *You need to spend 30 minutes (in) walking every morning.*

1. 為什麼不清理廚房？

_____

2. 為什麼不喝水？

_____

3. 她花了三天寫成這本書。

_____

4. 我們花五千元買這個錶。

_____

5. 為什麼不花五千元買這本字典？

_____

 Speaking Activities

Group Discussion

Form groups of four and discuss the following questions. Then, report your answers to the class.

1. For what do people run?

2. What equipment do we need for running or jogging?

3. What are the differences among running, jogging, and walking?

4. What are the similarities among running, jogging, and walking?

5. What advice did the writer of the text provide for walking?

Dialogue Practice

Invite a partner to practice the following dialogue.

Kathy: What sports do you like, Helen?

Helen: I like to play tennis. What about you?

Kathy: I like jogging because it is very easy.

Helen: How much time do you spend in jogging every week?

Kathy: About one hour. And you?

Helen: About two hours. However, sometimes I have difficulty finding a partner.

Kathy: That's why I like jogging. I can jog alone.

Helen: But it's more fun to play with friends.

Role Play

Imitate the dialogue above, and find a partner to talk about your favorite sport.

You play the part A.

A: (Ask what kind of sport your friend likes.)

B: (Answer A's question. Then ask what A likes.)

A: (Answer B's question. Ask B how much time she/he spends doing that sport.)

B: (Answer A's question. Ask A the same kind of question.)

A: (Answer B's question. Tell B what trouble you may have in playing this sport.)

B: (Tell A why you particularly like your sport.)

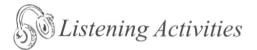 *Listening Activities*

Listen for the Main Idea

Listen to each dialogue or narration on the tape, and then according to what you hear on the tape, select the best answer to each question.

The setting is: A woman and a man are talking about controlling weight.

( ) 1. Which of the following is not related to what the speakers talk about?

　　(A) Controlling weight is not easy.

　　(B) Most people are not born runners.

　　(C) Walking is another way of weight control.

　　(D) The speakers are concerned with weight control.

( ) 2. Which of the following is not true?

　　(A) Walking is an inexpensive sport.

　　(B) Walking has the same benefits as jogging.

　　(C) Walking is a steady and continuous motion.

　　(D) Walking does not need a good plan.

( ) 3. What problem does the woman speaker have?

　　(A) She can't control her weight.

　　(B) She needs to put on some weight.

　　(C) She needs to go on a special diet.

　　(D) She needs exercise such as jogging and walking.

( ) 4. Why does the woman mean by saying "You need to set goals for yourself."?

　　(A) You must decide how much you'd like to spend on buying equipment.

　　(B) You must decide what you want to be in the future.

(C) You need to decide whether you want to be a professional athlete or not.

(D) You must make sure why you want to walk for exercise.

(   ) 5. What does the man speaker mean by saying "I just can't wait."?

(A) He is running out of time.

(B) He has something to do immediately.

(C) He would try using walking as a kind of exercise.

(D) He can't wait for the woman speaker to work together.

Writing Activities

Guided Writing

Complete each of the following.

1. Let us _____（為自由與民主而跑）.

2. The _____（把走路當運動的難題）is that it may rain.

3. Try increasing your running time _____（漸漸地／一點點地）.

4. If you want to get _____（你的健康）by _____
_____（控制飲食）, you need to _____（設定目標）
for yourself.

5. Many people do not _____（看待誠實）seriously.

Translation

Translate the following Chinese passage into English.

健康專家 (experts) 說人是會動的 (moving) 動物，[; but if they] 坐久了 [they] 變植物 (plants)，[; and if they] 躺久了 [they] 變礦物 (minerals)。所以運動對人是很重要的。走路是一種很容易做的運動，先 (first of all) 作好計畫，定好目標，持之 (do it)

以恆 (persistently)，慢慢地你就會很健康。

[Notes: The symbols [   ] indicate that you need to insert the suggested words and punctuation marks.]

_____

_____

_____

_____

_____

_____

_____

_____

_____

_____

_____

Unit Six

Are You an Eco-tourist?

 Pre-reading Activities

Recognize New Words

Learn the Chinese definition of each bold-faced word before you read the text.

1. **tourism**	觀光業
2. **popular**	普遍的
3. **affect**	影響
4. cause **damage**	破壞；傷害
5. **economic** effects	經濟的

6. **environmental** effects	環境的
7. **suggestions**	建議
8. an **eco-tourist**	講求環境保護的觀光客
9. public **transportation**	公共交通
10. traffic **congestion**	堵塞
11. an **enormous** problem	巨大的
12. **accommodation**	住宿
13. **remain**	保持
14. **out of season**	淡季
15. more **hospitable**	好客的
16. the **authorities**	權威當局
17. **adopt** the local lifestyle	採用

Brainstorming Questions

Discuss the following questions with your group members.

1. What preparations will you do before you go on a trip?

2. While visiting a foreign country, what should you care about?

3. What are your concerns when you are traveling?

4. Where can you find reference sources for your trip?

Read the text

Tourism around the world is so popular that in certain places it affects and even causes damage to the sights that the tourists have come to see. It is important to think about the economic, cultural, and environmental effects of being a tourist. So, before you go on vacation, here are some suggestions on how to be an eco-tourist. 5

1. Use public transportation. If everyone uses their cars, pollution and traffic congestion will become an enormous problem.

2. Stay in small hotels and eat local food. It's important that the money you spend on accommodation and food 10 remains within the local area.

3. Travel out of season. It's the best time to avoid crowds, and it's often cheaper, too.

4. Think of yourself as a guest, not a tourist. As a tourist, you're simply a source of money. 15

5. Learn the local language. If you make an effort to speak their language, you'll be able to talk to local people, and they are likely to be even more hospitable.

6. Be careful about taking photos. In some places, people are embarrassed when you take their photo. Find out 20 what the local custom is.

7. Find out about the place you're visiting. It's very impolite to the local people if you're only there because of the weather and don't want to know anything about where you are. 25

8. Use less water than at home. In certain places, the authorities supply the big hotels with water.

9. Use local guides. This will create jobs and help the local economy.

10. Adopt the local lifestyle. If you don't appreciate being in 30 a foreign country, why leave home in the first place?

Reading Comprehension Check

According to the text you read, answer the following questions.

( ) 1. If we can speak the local language when traveling, _____

    (A) we can buy the local things with lower prices.

    (B) we can live in the local hotels.

    (C) we can accept more respect from the local people.

    (D) local people will be more hospitable to us.

( ) 2. What is NOT the advantage of using the public transportation?

    (A) It can save more money.

    (B) It can help reduce air pollution.

    (C) You don't have to carry your own baggage.

    (D) It helps avoid traffic congestion.

( ) 3. "If you don't appreciate being in a foreign country, why leave home in the first place?" What does this sentence mean?

    (A) It means if we don't enjoy traveling, we should stay home.

    (B) It means we should do as Romans do.

    (C) It means we should not worry about spending money when traveling.

    (D) It means living in a foreign country is not as comfortable as at home.

( ) 4. What's the main theme of this article?

    (A) The writer wants readers to listen to his suggestions.

    (B) Tourism has become popular around the world.

    (C) Tourists always cause enormous problems to the place where they visit.

    (D) The writer tells readers how to become an eco-tourist.

( ) 5. According to the text, what does the prefix "eco-" mean?

    (A) It refers to ecology.

    (B) It refers to economy.

(C) It refers to both ecology and economics.

(D) There is insufficient information to predict what it means.

Developing Linguistic Ability

Vocabulary Growth

Learn the definition of the following words. Match them.

_____ 1. tourism   (A) sightseeing

_____ 2. popular   (B) money-making

_____ 3. affect   (C) surroundings

_____ 4. damage   (D) accept

_____ 5. economic   (E) power or right

_____ 6. environment   (F) keep on

_____ 7. suggestion   (G) overcrowding

_____ 8. transportation   (H) proposal

_____ 9. congestion   (I) harm or hurt

_____ 10. enormous   (J) sociable

_____ 11. accommodation   (K) very great

_____ 12. remain   (L) housing

_____ 13. hospitable   (M) conveyance

_____ 14. authorities   (N) have an influence

_____ 15. adopt   (O) well-liked

Words in Use

Select the best word to fill in the blank.

(   ) 1. Noise has _____ our living seriously. We become more impatient and angry easily.

(A) effects   (B) perfected   (C) affected   (D) impacts

(   ) 2. Tom has an _____ appetite. Before each meal, he eats two hamburgers and three fries.

(A) enough   (B) enormous   (C) economic   (D) aggressive

(   ) 3. The Lees are a _____ family. People like to stay with them.

(A) vigorous   (B) lively   (C) powerful   (D) hospitable

(   ) 4. When everyone else was in a panic, she _____ calm.

(A) remained   (B) felt   (C) became   (D) changed

(   ) 5. The committee finally _____ his proposal of giving listening tests on each monthly examination.

(A) admired   (B) adapted   (C) adopted   (D) advised

(   ) 6. Because of more and more protesters in front of the Presidential Office, the police exercised _____ to dispel protesters.

(A) permission   (B) authority   (C) rightness   (D) weight

(   ) 7. Hotel _____ is scarce in Kenting area during holidays, so we had better make a reservation in advance.

(A) transportation   (B) capacity

(C) occasion   (D) accommodation

(   ) 8. I don't want to go to Yangmingshan on Sundays because I will be caught in the traffic _____.

(A) convention   (B) congestion   (C) system   (D) block

(   ) 9. Every time I talk to my teacher, I often obtain valuable _____ from him.

(A) suggestions   (B) benefits   (C) pressures   (D) critics

(   ) 10. A happy family provides a loving _____ for its children.

(A) situation   (B) accommodation

(C) environment   (D) location

Increase Word Power–Synonyms

Give one synonym for each of the following words.

_____ 1. enormous   (A) sociable

_____ 2. hospitable   (B) hurt

_____ 3. economic   (C) great

_____ 4. damage   (D) stay

_____ 5. remain   (E) thrifty

                                 (F) costly

Increase Word Power–Antonyms

Give one antonym for each of the following words.

_____ 1. enormous   (A) expensive

_____ 2. economic   (B) tiny

_____ 3. local   (C) luxurious

_____ 4. cheap   (D) foreign

_____ 5. careful   (E) careless

                                 (F) domestic

Developing Grammatical Competence

Grammatical Features

Learn the following structures.

Pattern One   **so + Adj./Adv. + that**

Pattern Two   **It's important that-clause**

Pattern Three   **It's the best time to VP**

Pattern Four   **As a NP, you are....**

Try to complete each of the following with your own words.

1. The test is so difficult _____

2. It's important that the government _____

3. It's the best time to _____

4. As a _____, you are _____

5. As a _____, you need _____

6. It's the best chance to _____

7. It is necessary that we _____

8. The traffic is so _____ that _____

9. As a _____, we realize that _____

Cloze Exercise

Select the best answer to fill in the blank.

With the advancement of transportation and the ___1___ of living standards, tourism ___2___ the world is more and more popular. However, tourists are ___3___ for the damage ___4___ they have done to the sights. So, ___5___ a civilized tourist, you have to take the economic, cultural, and environmental effects ___6___ consideration before ___7___ a trip. ___8___, before you go on your vacation, you must keep economic, cultural ___9___ ecological concern in ___10___ when you are designing your trip.

( ) 1. (A) increase   (B) improvement   (C) expand   (D) enlarge

( ) 2. (A) around   (B) about   (C) along   (D) aside

( ) 3. (A) impossible   (B) responsible   (C) regretful   (D) thankful

( ) 4. (A) why   (B) who   (C) where   (D) that

( ) 5. (A) it being   (B) being   (C) such as   (D) like

( ) 6. (A) into   (B) at   (C) with   (D) for

( ) 7. (A) undergoing   (B) overtaking   (C) overdoing   (D) undertaking

(   )   8. (A) Similarly   (B) That is   (C) However   (D) Likewise

(   )   9. (A) such as   (B) as well as   (C) or   (D) also

(   ) 10. (A) determination (B) heart   (C) mind   (D) brain

Speaking Activities

Survey

Go around the class and ask 2 people the questions in the following survey. Write down "Yes" or "No" to each question and take notes.

Example:

A: When you travel, do you use public transportation?

B: No, I don't.

A: Why not?

B: It may be cheaper, but it's always crowded.

	Name 1 (Y/N), Notes	Name 2 (Y/N), Notes
When you travel, do you...? 1. use public transportation		
2. stay in small hotels and eat local food		
3. usually travel out of season		
4. think of yourself as a guest, not a tourist		
5. learn the local language before starting off		
6. care about taking photos of others		
7. find out about the place you're visiting in advance		
8. use less water than at home		
9. use local tour guides		
10. adopt the local lifestyle for more enjoyment		

Group Discussion

Form groups of four and discuss the following questions. Then, report your answers to the class.

1. Would you like to travel as an eco-tourist? Why or why not?

2. What advice would you give to someone who wants to travel like an eco-tourist?

3. Would you rather stay in a tourist hotel or a small local hotel? Why?

4. If you join a tour group, is it possible to follow what the writer suggests in the text? Why or why not?

 # *Listening Activities*

Lecture Comprehension Practice

You will hear a mini-lecture on the tape. It's about being an eco-tourist. Listen carefully, and then try to complete each of the following.

(　) 1. To be an eco-tourist, first of all, you have to pay attention _____

    (A) to the local customs and practices.

    (B) to the local transportation and facilities.

    (C) to the local people and families.

(　) 2. Being an eco-tourist, you have to adapt yourself _____

    (A) to the new working environment.

    (B) to the new climate pattern.

    (C) to the local lifestyle.

(　) 3. Local people may feel embarrassed when you _____

    (A) ask them questions on the streets.

    (B) take photos of them without asking for permission.

    (C) talk to them using impolite words or behave impolitely.

(   ) 4. You will be more welcome if you can _____

       (A) entertain the local people at the local restaurants.

       (B) speak the local language and respect their culture.

       (C) bring gifts to them and give a party to them.

(   ) 5. You can fully and better understand the place where you visit by taking

       advantage of _____

       (A) local resources and public facilities.

       (B) public transportation to go where people want to go.

       (C) local people who know where to take you to visit.

(   ) 6. The purpose of staying in a small local hotel instead of a tourist hotel is

       _____

       (A) to experience the local lifestyle.

       (B) to get a better local view.

       (C) to stay as close as the local people.

Writing Activities

Sentence Transformation

Follow the given examples. Try to combine two or three sentences into one.

Example 1:

1a. To study English is necessary.

1b. We study English.

→ *It is necessary for us to study English.*

→ *It is necessary that we study English.*

Example 2:

2a. It is impolite.

2b. That you talk rudely to a lady is impolite.

→ *It is impolite for you to talk rudely to a lady.*

→ *It is impolite that you talk rudely to a lady.*

3a. It is reasonable.

3b. That you help your brothers and sisters is reasonable.

→ _____

→ _____

4a. To learn computer skills is necessary.

4b. Students should learn computer skills.

→ _____

→ _____

5a. It is ridiculous.

5b. That we learn a foreign language by memorizing a dictionary is ridiculous.

→ _____

→ _____

6a. To understand cultural differences is important.

6b. Tourists should understand cultural differences.

→ _____

→ _____

7a. To learn vocabulary is essential.

7b. We should learn vocabulary when we learn a foreign language.

→ _____

→ _____

Correct Grammatical Errors

Correct all the grammatical errors in bold-faced words and put the corrections in the blanks.

By the advancement of transportation, tourism around the world is more and more popular. **Therefore**, it's responsible **about** the damage to the sights that visitors have come to see. **As being** a civilized tourist, it's important **of** you to take **economy**, cultural, and environmental effects **from** consideration before **undertake** a trip. Here **is** some suggestions on **where** to be an eco-tourist.

1. _____   2. _____   3. _____

4. _____   5. _____   6. _____

7. _____   8. _____   9. _____

10. _____

Sentence Completion

Use your own words to complete each of the following.

1. _____ around the world is so _____ that we can _____.

2. It is important to think about _____ when we talk about tourism.

3. If everyone uses _____, traffic congestion will _____.

4. It's important that _____.

5. As a _____, you can _____.

6. Make an effort to _____, and you will _____ _____.

7. _____ are embarrassed when _____

_____ .

8. It's very impolite to _____ .

9. They don't know anything about where _____ .

10. If you don't appreciate being _____ , why do you

_____ ?

Paragraph Writing

Within 60 words write a paragraph on the issues raised in the following question.
What are your concerns on the economic, cultural, or environmental effects of
local tourism?

_____

_____

_____

_____

_____

_____

_____

_____

_____

_____

_____

_____

_____

_____

_____

_____

_____

_____

_____

_____

_____

_____

_____

_____

_____

_____

_____

~A friend in need is a friend indeed.

Accepting Compliments

 Pre-reading Activities

Recognize New Words

Learn the Chinese definition of each bold-faced word before you read the text.

1. accept **compliments**	恭維；讚許
2. **a pat on the back**	鼓勵
3. be **shrugged off**	一笑置之；不理會
4. a **fantastic** car	神奇的，美妙的
5. **downplay** compliments	低調處理；輕描淡寫地處理

6. **give the credit to** someone   歸功於

7. **react to** compliments   反應

8. make a **derogatory remark**   貶低他人的評論

9. show **humility**   謙虛

10. receive a gift with **gratitude**   感激

11. **give recognition to** employees   給予肯定；承認…

12. **maintain morale**   維持士氣

13. **assure workers' performance**   肯定員工的表現

Brainstorming Questions

Discuss the following questions with your group members.

1. When someone compliments you, how do you react to that?

2. Do foreigners such as Americans accept compliments the way you do?

3. Why is accepting compliments more difficult than giving compliments?

Read the Text

Everyone needs a pat on the back now and then, but compliments are often easier to give than to receive, especially for Americans. Tell an American that he or she plays a great game of tennis, and the compliment will probably be shrugged off with "It must be my lucky day" or "This new racket is wonderful"   5 or "My tennis teacher is fantastic!" Of course, a person might also smile and say "Thank you," but many Americans downplay compliments by giving the credit to someone or something else.

It is interesting to compare how people from different cultures react to compliments. In some countries, if you   10 compliment someone on a possession, he or she will give it to you or tell you that you may use it whenever you like. In some countries, a person will make a derogatory remark about it or show humility and unworthiness of praise. But in most cultures, compliments are received with gratitude.   15

A current form of complimenting is referred to as stroking, the praise or positive feedback people give each other, especially at the workplace. American companies understand the importance of giving recognition to employees in order to maintain morale and assure workers' performance. Companies   20 often give rewards for outstanding achievement and service.

Reading Comprehension Check

According to the text you read, answer the following questions.

(　　) 1. What's the main theme of this article?

　　　(A) Companies should give recognition to their employees.

　　　(B) Accepting compliments is more difficult than giving compliments.

　　　(C) Accepting compliments is culturally related.

　　　(D) People like accepting compliments more than giving compliments.

(　　) 2. What does the word "stroking" mean in the last paragraph?

　　　(A) It's a way of rejecting praise or positive feedback at the workplace.

　　　(B) It's a polite way to decline compliments from people who seldom give compliments to others.

　　　(C) It's the way to accept positive feedback when people give compliments to us.

　　　(D) It's a current form of mutual praise or positive feedback found at the workplace.

(　)　3. Which of the following is true?

(A) In few countries people accept compliments with gratitude.

(B) In most countries people accept compliments with gratitude.

(C) In most cultures gratitude is given when compliments are given.

(D) In some countries gratitude and compliments are accepted equally.

(　)　4. How do Americans accept compliments given to them?

(A) They downplay compliments by giving the credit to someone or something else.

(B) They decline compliments by recognizing the performance or work of others.

(C) They regard it as a great honor especially when it is treated as an honor.

(D) They give credits to others who may not be worthy of accepting compliments.

(　)　5. In what area will this article be possibly found?

(A) In social studies.

(B) In natural sciences.

(C) In anthropological studies.

(D) In cultural studies.

(　)　6. What's the meaning of "react" in the second paragraph? It means "_____."

(A) respond　(B) rebut　(C) recall　(D) reflect

(　)　7. The phrase "a current form" means "_____."

(A) an outdated form　(B) a fashionable style

(C) a present style　(D) a type of electric power

(　)　8. The main theme of this article is _____.

(A) to tell why we should not receive compliments from others

(B) to explain the relationship between accepting compliments and culture

(C) to explain why Americans sound fantastic in accepting compliments

(D) to illustrate how to accept and react to compliments

( ) 9. When your friends say "You look very attractive," what is a proper way to react to that?

(A) Watch out your derogatory words.

(B) It must be my lucky day.

(C) Where, where.

(D) Thank you for your compliments.

Developing Linguistic Ability

Recogzine New Words

Read the definitions, and choose the best word to fill in the blank.

( ) 1. _____: a sport instrument with a round or oval stringed frame （球拍）

(A) packet   (B) rocket   (C) pocket   (D) racket

( ) 2. _____: wonderful or marvelous （奇佳的）

(A) fantastic   (B) fanatic   (C) frantic   (D) frank

( ) 3. _____: no worthiness or merit at all （沒價值；沒優點）

(A) unworthiness   (B) unwarranted   (C) pledge   (D) privilege

( ) 4. _____: present, happening now （現今的，現行的）

(A) pleasant   (B) popular   (C) continuous (D) current

( ) 5. _____: to express approval or admiration （稱讚；表揚）

(A) praise   (B) raise   (C) adore   (D) reduce

( ) 6. _____: to make certain; ensure （使確定；保證）

(A) treasure   (B) pressure   (C) assure   (D) measure

(　　) 7. ＿＿＿＿＿＿＿: to make seem less important than it really is（減低…重要性；輕視）

     (A) cherish   (B) disregard   (C) downplay   (D) value

(　　) 8. ＿＿＿＿＿＿＿: the feeling of being grateful, thankfulness（感激，感謝）

     (A) gratitude   (B) graduation   (C) grant   (D) greed

(　　) 9. ＿＿＿＿＿＿＿: showing a hostile or critical attitude（貶低的，毀損的）

     (A) derogatory   (B) democracy   (C) demand   (D) denounce

(　　) 10. ＿＿＿＿＿＿＿: response or information reacting to a stimulus（反饋訊息）

     (A) formula   (B) feedback   (C) frank   (D) fetch

(　　) 11. ＿＿＿＿＿＿＿: showing confidence and optimism（樂觀的；積極的）

     (A) promise   (B) pessimistic   (C) passive   (D) positive

(　　) 12. ＿＿＿＿＿＿＿: action or achievement（成就；表現）

     (A) performance   (B) production   (C) acting   (D) show

(　　) 13. ＿＿＿＿＿＿＿: state of confidence, enthusiasm, determination（士氣；精神狀態）

     (A) moral   (B) morality   (C) morale   (D) mortal

(　　) 14. ＿＿＿＿＿＿＿: likely to happen; possibly（可能地）

     (A) proportionally   (B) properly   (C) probably   (D) patiently

(　　) 15. ＿＿＿＿＿＿＿: to respond; reply; answer（反應；回應）

     (A) backpack   (B) reward   (C) retaliate   (D) react

Words in Use

Select the most proper word to fill in the blank to complete each of the following sentences.

(　　) 1. He ＿＿＿＿＿＿＿ the dancer on her skillful performance.

(A) shrugged off   (B) complimented   (C) downplayed   (D) reacted

( ) 2. My manager is late, and I guess he is _____ stuck in a traffic jam.

(A) entirely   (B) actually   (C) thoroughly   (D) probably

( ) 3. The traffic problem in the city is serious and it can't be _____ as if it didn't exist.

(A) reacted to   (B) referred to   (C) shrugged off (D) pushed off

( ) 4. Timmy's parents were _____ when he did not return home on time.

(A) frantic   (B) fascinated   (C) fragile   (D) fantastic

( ) 5. The manager gave all his _____ to those who offered help.

(A) strength   (B) belief   (C) credit   (D) trust

( ) 6. _____ to other's questions properly is not so easy.

(A) Due   (B) Expecting   (C) Owing   (D) Reacting

( ) 7. The mean person always makes remarks that are highly _____.

(A) incredible   (B) dispensable   (C) derogatory   (D) trustable

( ) 8. My professor is a humble person, He always treats people with _____.

(A) humor   (B) humility   (C) humidity   (D) humanity

( ) 9. I'm sure that I don't deserve so much _____.

(A) prize   (B) award   (C) praise   (D) rewards

( ) 10. The company needs more _____ from consumers to improve their goods.

(A) backpack   (B) wash-back   (C) cutback   (D) feedback

( ) 11. My brother shows a _____ attitude toward life.

(A) active   (B) relative   (C) positive   (D) subjective

( ) 12. Our government offered an award in _____ of her contributions.

(A) reception   (B) institution   (C) tuition   (D) recognition

(   ) 13. This news is good for boosting the baseball team's _____.

       (A) moral   (B) morale   (C) morality   (D) mortal

(   ) 14. The Dragon-Dance _____ begins at eight o'clock tonight.

       (A) performance   (B) tradition   (C) display   (D) festival

(   ) 15. The scientist, frequently _____ to as the King of Discovery, is my friend.

       (A) shrugged   (B) reacted   (C) referred   (D) responded

Increase Word Power–Synonyms

Match the words that are semantically related.

Group A

_____ 1. strike (*v.*)   (A) download

_____ 2. current   (B) hit

_____ 3. praise (*v.*)   (C) prevalent; present

_____ 4. gratitude   (D) recognition

_____ 5. credit   (E) thankfulness; appreciation

                          (F) extol; commend

Group B

_____ 6. derogatory   (G) brilliant; prominent

_____ 7. feedback   (H) spirit; enthusiasm

_____ 8. positive   (I) compliment

_____ 9. outstanding   (J) guarantee; pledge

_____10. achievement   (K) response; reaction

_____11. morale   (L) optimistic

_____12. assure

(M) belittling; unfavorable

(N) success

Increase Word Power–Antonyms

Match the words that are semantically opposite.

Group A

_____ 1. current

_____ 2. praise

_____ 3. gratitude

_____ 4. downplay

_____ 5. humility

_____ 6. derogatory

(A) brag

(B) emphasize

(C) appreciative

(D) ingratitude

(E) outdated; obsolete

(F) criticize

(G) prevalent

Group B

_____ 7. positive

_____ 8. rewards

_____ 9. outstanding

_____10. achievement

_____11. assure

_____12. probably

(H) punishment

(I) impossibly; unlikely

(J) ordinary; commonplace

(K) negative

(L) failure

(M) suspect, doubt

Text Review through Cloze Test

According to the text you read, select the best answer to fill in the blank.

Giving compliments or praising somebody is very cultural. It can't be denied ___1___ giving praises is much easier than receiving them. ___2___, this is because most people like to be complimented. For instance, most of Americans

___3___ the compliments by means of contributing credit ___4___ someone else. Similarly, most of Chinese may ___5___ reject your compliments by downplaying ___6___. Sometimes we may find a person who might say "thank you" or simply ___7___ your compliments cheerfully when he or she is complimented. The ___8___ to the compliments differ from one culture to another ___9___. Therefore, when learning a second language, we need to learn not only linguistic knowledge ___10___ also communicative competence which includes cultural knowledge.

( ) 1. (A) when   (B) why   (C) because   (D) that

( ) 2. (A) In fact   (B) However   (C) Therefore   (D) As a result

( ) 3. (A) downplay   (B) upgrade   (C) deserve   (D) reject

( ) 4. (A) to   (B) for   (C) from   (D) of

( ) 5. (A) preliminarily   (B) cheerfully   (C) humbly   (D) reluctantly

( ) 6. (A) themselves   (B) friends   (C) companions   (D) partners

( ) 7. (A) contribute   (B) accept   (C) distribute   (D) intercept

( ) 8. (A) promotions   (B) restrictions   (C) reactions   (D) presentation

( ) 9. (A) as well   (B) either   (C) type   (D) friend

( ) 10. (A) and   (B) or   (C) as   (D) but

Morphology

In the following you will learn three ways to derive a new word from the given word.

1. To form a "Noun" from a "Verb", we can add the suffix {-ment} to the end of the verb. Give a noun form for each of the following verbs.

(1) achieve _____   (4) accomplish _____

(2) treat _____   (5) equip _____

(3) establish _____

2. **To form a "Noun" from a "Verb", we may also add the suffix {-ance} to the end of the verb. Give a noun form for each of the following verbs.**

(1) maintain _____   (4) accept _____

(2) perform _____   (5) guide _____

(3) disturb _____

3. **One way to form a "Noun" from an "Adjective" is to add the suffix {-ness} to the end of the adjective. Give the noun form for each of the following.**

(1) worthy _____   (4) busy _____

(2) useful _____   (5) lazy _____

(3) happy _____

Structural Completion

Some verbs have to be followed by certain types of prepositions. Complete each of the following by filling in one proper preposition in the blank.

Notes: Beware of the prepositions that are used after the verbs in the following sentences.

1. Many people received compliments from friends _____ gratitude.

2. We may try to shrug _____ the unfair comments on us.

3. People from different cultures react _____ hugging differently.

4. The teacher gave rewards to students _____ their outstanding performance.

5. Shrugging your shoulders is usually referred _____ as refusing or denying.

Idiom or Phrase Drill

Match the phrases in the left column with the proper definitions given in the right column.

Part A: Matching

_____ 1. shrug off

_____ 2. a pat on the back

_____ 3. react to

_____ 4. compliment someone

_____ 5. give recognition to

(A) a praise, or encouragement

(B) say nice words to someone

(C) deny; treat as an unimportant thing

(D) accept

(E) respond to

(F) speak ill of someone

Part B: Sentence Completion

Select a proper phrase to complete each of the following sentences. You need to adjust some word forms. Each phrase is used only once.

give compliments to	give recognition to	pat on my shoulder
compare...with	shrug off	compliment...on
have many possessions	be compared to	react to
derogatory words	good remarks	whenever you can
it is unworthy of	show humility	receive...with gratitude
be referred to as	give the credit to	give rewards to...for

1. The sun is often _____ the center of the universe.

2. Gambling is often _____ playing with fire.

3. How do you _____ Chinese _____ English?

4. He's an alcoholic. _____ stopping him from drinking.

5. The teacher _____ when she complimented me.

6. My parents _____ my hard-work.

7. Foreign countries _____ Taiwan for her democracy.

8. Most countries _____ Taiwan _____ her economic success.

9. Humble people tend to _____ when they are given compliments.

10. People with good manners never use _____.

11. The professor gave very _____ on her term paper.

12. How did Taiwanese _____ China's missile exercise?

13. Children should _____ gifts from parents _____.

14. James _____ when his coach complimented him on his excellent performance in the tennis match.

15. Our principal _____ us _____ our outstanding projects.

 Speaking Activities

Group Discussion

Form groups of four and discuss the following questions. Then, report your answers to the class.

1. When someone says "You did a wonderful job" to you, how would you react to the compliment?

2. According to the writer, how do Americans react to the compliments they receive?

3. When your friend tells you that your dress looks beautiful, what would you say to him or her in return?

4. From the passage, *Accepting Compliments*, what have you learned about accepting compliments?

Dialogue Drill

Invite a partner to practice the following dialogue. You play the part B, and your partner plays the part A. Change the role later on.

A: You look so great today!

B: _____

A: This red dress really looks great on you.

B: _____

A: Where did you get it?

B: _____

A: Do you usually get your new dress there?

B: _____

A: I think you must have a good taste in choosing dresses.

B: _____

Listening Activities

Text Comprehension Practice

Listen to the passage on the tape carefully and answer all the questions that you read in your book.

(   ) 1. According to the passage you hear, what is essential in social life?

    (A) Having good social status.   (B) Having much money.

    (C) Giving compliments.   (D) Giving condemnation.

(   ) 2. From this passage, we learn giving praises is _____ receiving them.

    (A) easier than   (B) harder than

    (C) the same as   (D) more important than

(   ) 3. The reactions to compliments that people have may _____

    (A) differ from culture to culture.   (B) make no difference.

    (C) differ from a place to another.   (D) depend on situations.

(   ) 4. A second language learner should master _____

       (A) both cultural and linguistic knowledge.

       (B) only cultural knowledge prior to others.

       (C) only linguistic knowledge prior to others.

       (D) either cultural or linguistic knowledge.

(   ) 5. According to the passage you hear, which of the following is true?

       (A) Americans react to compliments by downplaying themselves.

       (B) Chinese react to compliments by downplaying themselves.

       (C) Americans seldom contribute credit to their friends.

       (D) Chinese people do not react to compliments properly.

Conversation Comprehension Practice

Listen to the dialogue on the tape, and according to what you hear on the tape, answer all the questions given below.

1. What did the two speakers talk about at the beginning?

   They _____

2. According to this dialogue, what do you think of accepting compliments?

   Accepting compliments differs _____

3. When you are complimented by someone, how will you react to that?

   _____

4. Do you think the female speaker is smart and attractive? Why or why not?

   _____

5. Do you think the male speaker is teasing or complimenting the female speaker? Give your reasons.

   _____

Dialogue Comprehension

Listen to the dialogue on the tape, then answer the questions that follow.

Situation: Tom and Jerry are having a small talk with each other after a tennis game.

1. When did this dialogue take place?

   It took place _____

2. How did Jerry react to Tom's compliments?

   Jerry thought that _____

3. How could you tell that Tom was not complimenting Jerry?

   _____

4. What possible relationship between the two can you predict?

   They _____

Writing Activities

Identifying Structural Errors

There are some expressions marked from (A), (B), (C) through (L) in the following passage. Some of them are correct and some are incorrect. Give corrections in the blanks. If there is no error, put "correct" in the blank.

Many Americans shrugging off their compliments with smiling. Sometimes they
          (A)   (B)

downplayed compliments to give the credit to someone or something of
    (C)   (D)   (E)

others. We know it is easy to give compliments than accepting them. To learn
                (F)   (G)

what to accept compliments is important and necessary. It is worthiness of
  (H)   (I)   (J)

learning how to accept compliment.
  (K)   (L)

Answers:

A: _____ B: _____ C: _____ D: _____

E: _____ F: _____ G: _____ H: _____

I: _____ J: _____ K: _____ L: _____

Translation

Translate each of the following into English.

1. 他恭維我的時候拍著我的肩膀。

   He _____ when he _____ me.

2. 她肯定我的網球技術。

   She gives _____ to me _____ tennis skills.

3. 我們的老師讚美我們的成功演出。

   Our teacher _____ us _____ our _____ performance.

4. 你能比較中英文化嗎？

   Can you _____ the Chinese culture _____ the English culture?

5. 聽到別人的恭維話你的反應如何？

   Upon hearing _____ from people, how do you _____ them?

6. 不要把有價值的財物放在家裡。

   Don't keep valuable _____ at home.

7. 他太懶了，鼓勵他沒用（不值得）。

   He's too lazy. It is _____ encouraging him.

8. Edison 常常被指（視）為發明之父。

   Edison is often _____ the father of inventions.

9. 對別人的詢問做出適當的反應不是很容易。

It is not easy to _____ properly _____ the inquiries from people.

10. 大部分新聞報導對這次意外事件輕描淡寫，一筆帶過。

Most news reports _____ the accident.

11. 他對人生抱持著正面積極的態度。

He has a _____ toward life.

12. 我們需要從消費者得到反饋訊息以提高產品品質。

We need consumers' _____ to raise the _____ of our products.

13. 他因為傑出的能力而獲得升遷的機會。

He had a chance of _____ because of his _____ ability.

14. 這是一個嚴重的問題，不能當作它不存在而不理不睬。

This is a serious problem and it can't be _____ as if it didn't exist.

15. 我的老闆總是說出極傷人的話。

My boss always makes remarks that are highly _____.

16. 她終生感激他的救命之恩。

She felt eternal _____ to him for saving her life.

17. 這好消息對提高全隊的士氣有好處。

This news is good for boosting the team's _____.

Paragraph Development

Use the given Chinese hints to develop a paragraph. Before that, try to answer the following questions and use them as guiding procedures.

1. What is the main topic of the first paragraph of the text you read? (What's the topic sentence?)

Compliments are _____.

2. How did the writer support this topic? (Choose one answer.)

(A) By giving explanations.

(B) By giving examples.

(C) By showing a contrast.

3. The main idea that compliments are easier to give than to receive is supported by two incidents. What are these two incidents (reasons)?

_____

_____

段落寫作練習開始

〔⋯〕表示思考方式；（⋯）表示語意並把它譯成英文；（1, 2, 3, ...）表示發展順序。

(1)〔主題句〕（給予恭維比接受容易。）(2)〔說明原因支持主題句〕（我們可以容易地稱讚別人的成就。）(3)〔舉例說明原因支持主題句〕（我們也可以容易地稱讚別人的美麗外表。）(4)〔舉另一理由支持主題句〕（在稱讚別人的時候，我們可以毫無困難地找出適當的詞句來讚美別人。）(5)〔從反方面說明原因來支持主題句〕（但是在別人稱讚我們的時候，我們常常找不到適當的詞句來回應別人的讚美。）(6)〔舉例說明支持主題句〕（例如，別人讚美我們的房子很漂亮時，我們真的不知道如何回答。）(7)〔結論句來呼應主題句〕（顯然的，回應別人的恭維要比恭維別人困難很多。）

_____

_____

_____

_____

_____

_____

_____

Unit Eight

Do-It-Yourself

 Pre-reading Activities

Recognize New Words

Learn the Chinese definition of each bold-faced word before you read the text.

1. household **repairs**	修理
2. professional **carpenters**	木工
3. **plumbers**	水管工
4. light **switches**	開關
5. **water heaters**	熱水器

6. see **videocassettes**	錄影帶
7. build **cabinets**	木櫃
8. **install** windows	裝設
9. **wax** wooden floors	打蠟
10. build **porches**	走廊
11. **hardware** stores	五金
12. an electric **saw**	電鋸
13. **shovels and wrenches**	鏟子及扳手
14. at **discount prices**	折扣價
15. **assemble furniture**	組合傢俱
16. **lawnmowers**	割草機
17. **amateur** electricians	業餘的

Brainstorming Questions

Discuss the following questions with your group members.

1. Suppose the water pipe of your house is broken, and you can not find a plumber to fix it for you. What are you going to do about it?

2. What does DIY stand for?

3. What are the advantages of DIY?

4. How can we apply the concept of DIY to language learning?

5. Share your experience of DIY with friends.

Read the Text

Many homeowners hire contractors to do their household repairs. Professional painters paint the inside of homes. Professional carpenters fix steps and repair doors. Plumbers fix problems with toilets and sinks. And electricians repair problems with light switches and water heaters. However, many 5 homeowners do these types of repairs themselves. They enjoy the work so much that many of them do their own home improvements, too.

There are many resources available that make these kinds of do-it-yourself jobs easy to do. Book stores and libraries carry 10 many books and magazines that offer suggestions and ideas for home repairs and improvements. There are also videocassettes and TV shows that give complete instructions for building cabinets, putting tile in bathrooms, installing windows, and even building additional rooms to enlarge a home. There are also 15 programs that show how to wax wooden floors, clean fireplaces, and paint decorative designs on walls. Local colleges and high schools offer adult education classes in the evenings and on weekends. In these classes, people can learn such things as techniques for building furniture and porches, ways to set up a 20 solar heating system, and procedures for saving energy in the home.

When homeowners are ready to begin their projects, they can go to their neighborhood hardware store to find many of the tools and supplies they need. These small stores sell all kinds of 25 tools—from hammers and saws to shovels and wrenches. They also carry electrical wire, paintbrushes, toilet parts, and many types of wallpaper and colors of house paint.

Some hardware stores are larger than the typical neighborhood store. They look like warehouses and sell many 30 things at discount prices. In addition to the merchandise available at the smaller hardware stores, most of these larger stores also sell doors, windows, easy-to-assemble furniture, and lumber. Some also carry large plants and trees and other big items, such as lawnmowers and children's swing sets. Cus- 35 tomers can get a lot of help at these large stores. There are guidebooks on wallpapering, housepainting, carpentry, plumbing, and electrical wiring.The employees are usually happy to offer information and suggestions.

With a few necessary tools, some good instructions, and a 40 little patience, do-it-yourself homeowners can become amateur electricians, plumbers, carpenters, and painters. Finishing a household repair or improvement gives them a great sense of accomplishment and the satisfaction of learning a new skill. And since they pay for only the materials and not for the labor, do-it- 45 yourself homeowners are happy to see how much money they can save!

Reading Comprehension Check

According to the text you read, answer the following questions.

1. Contractors can help homeowners with _____

2. Professional carpenters can help homeowners with _____

3. Similarly, plumbers can fix problems with _____

4. If your lights in the living room are out of order, you hire _____

   to _____

5. The reference sources of keeping household can be found in _____

6. People in America can learn _____ to maintain

their houses by attending adult education classes.

7. In a hardware store people can find things such as _____

8. If you don't hire a contractor to do repairs for you, you can learn the skills by

_____

9. An example of Do-It-Yourself guidebook is _____

10. At least two advantages of DIY are (1) _____, and

(2) _____

Developing Linguistic Ability

Vocabulary Recognition

Learn the definition of the following words. Match them.

Group A

_____ 1. homeowner   (A) concerned with the management of a house

_____ 2. contractor   (B) a person whose job is to fit and repair water pipes

_____ 3. household   (C) to set (an apparatus) up, ready for use

_____ 4. plumber   (D) any of the possessions or qualities of a person, an

_____ 5. electrician   organization

_____ 6. water heater   (E) the person who owns the house

_____ 7. improvement   (F) a person or company that contracts to do work or

_____ 8. resource   provide supplies in large amounts

_____ 9. available   (G) a machine to heat water

_____ 10. install   (H) the act of improving

(I) a person whose job is to fit and repair electrical

    apparatus

(J) able to be got, obtained, used, seen, etc.

Group B

_____ 11. enlarge   (K) to cause to grow larger or wider

_____ 12. decorative   (L) thin mental in the form of a thread

_____ 13. porch   (M) a large building for storing things, esp. things that are to be sold

_____ 14. hardware   (N) used for decorating

_____ 15. shovel   (O) to gather or collect into a group or into one place

_____ 16. wire   (P) things for sale; goods

_____ 17. warehouse   (Q) a machine which can be pushed or driven along the ground to cut grass

_____ 18. assemble   (R) equipment and tools for the home and garden

_____ 19. merchandise   (S) a tool with a broad usu. square or rounded blade fixed to a handle

_____ 20. lawnmower   (T) a roofed entrance built out from a house or church

Group C

_____ 21. wax   (U) fulfillment of a need, desire, etc.

_____ 22. procedure   (V) a person who does something for enjoyment and without being paid for it

_____ 23. discount   (W) the act of accomplishing or finishing work completely and successfully

_____ 24. amateur

_____ 25. accomplishment   (X) a set of actions necessary for doing something

_____ 26. satisfaction   (Y) a reduction made in the cost of buying goods

     (Z) to put wax on

Words in Use

From the word lists (given in Group A, B, C) above select one proper word to fill in the blank in the following.

1. _____ can be landlords because they have houses for rent.

2. We need a _____ to build the new factory.

3. We may get some parts for the _____ to fix pipes.

4. The light is out. Go find an _____ .

5. Turn on the _____ if you want to take a hot shower.

6. Some house _____ are needed after the quake.

7. Oil is one of the most natural _____ in the world.

8. Those shoes are not _____ in your size.

9. We're having central heating system _____ in the building.

10. There is no sun if you stay in the _____ .

11. Students store their things in the _____ at the school end.

12. The grass in the garden is long. Take the _____ to cut the grass.

13. Can you _____ the car for me while I'm busy?

14. _____ for using this machine are very important.

15. The department store has a _____ now; you may go to try your luck.

Synonyms

Give a semantically related word to each of the following. Match them.

Group A

_____ 1. decorative   A. goods

_____ 2. install   B. put together

_____ 3. warehouse   C. clothes factory

_____ 4. assemble   D. ornamental

_____ 5. merchandise   E. equip

                          F. storage house

Group B

_____ 6. homeowner   G. fulfillment

_____ 7. household   H. ritual

_____ 8. wax   I. candle

_____ 9. procedure   J. polish

_____ 10. accomplishment   K. domestic

                                      L. landlord

Antonyms

Match words that have opposite meanings.

_____ 1. amateur   A. tenant

_____ 2. satisfaction   B. shrink

_____ 3. assemble   C. professional

_____ 4. enlarge   D. tear

_____ 5. homeowner   E. dissatisfaction

                                      F. dismantle

Words for Fun: Morphology

Follow the instructions to create words.

A. Making compound words:

    Example: home-_____ →homeowner; hometown; homework

1. house-_____   (1) _____   (2) _____   (3) _____

2. store-_____   (1) _____   (2) _____   (3) _____

3. _____-holder   (1) _____   (2) _____   (3) _____

4. _____-ware   (1) _____   (2) _____   (3) _____

5. _____-wear   (1) _____   (2) _____   (3) _____

B. Matching a rhyme: Give 3 words that rhyme the same as the underlined part of the given word.

1. compli**ment**   (1) _____   (2) _____   (3) _____

2. r**oom**   (1) _____   (2) _____   (3) _____

3. proced**ure**   (1) _____   (2) _____   (3) _____

4. inst**all**   (1) _____   (2) _____   (3) _____

5. w**ax**   (1) _____   (2) _____   (3) _____

 Speaking Activities

Group Discussion

According to the text you read, discuss the answers to the following questions.
Report your answers to the class.

1. List five resources available for do-it-yourself jobs.

2. Who do homeowners hire if they don't do it themselves?

3. Where can homeowners find the tools and supplies they need?

4. Why do so many homeowners want to do it themselves?

5. What kind of feelings will they have if they finish a household repair or improvement?

Role Play

Try to act out the following dialogue.

Imagine that you are a homeowner. The windows in your house are broken. You need to go to the hardware store to find some tools, but you can't find the things you need in the store. Now, create a conversation between you and the storekeeper.

A: Excuse me. (Ask where you can find window glass.)

B: It's over there, in Isle Number Eight.

A: (Ask how they charge the glass.)

B: What size do you need? We charge by size.

A: (Tell you need a size of 3 feet by 5 feet.)

B: Sorry we don't have that size.

A: (Ask what size is available.)

B: We can cut the size for you.

A: (Ask how much they charge for the cutting.)

B: One dollar for the cutting.

A: (Ask how much it will cost in total.)

B: That will be fifty-one dollars.

A: (Ask where you can pay.)

B: Pay to the cashier. Go straight from here and you will find it.

Conversation Practice

First, from the choices given below the text choose the best answers to complete the conversation. Then, find a partner to practice the following conversation.

Greg: Hey, Tim. What are you doing here? Long time no see. What's up?

Tim: Hello, Greg. _____1_____ What's new? I think the time we saw each other last time is about two years ago.

Greg: Yes, _____2_____ Why are you here?

Tim: Well, do you know the guestroom in our house?

Greg: Yes, what's wrong with it?

Tim: The floor of that room needs repairs.

Greg: _____3_____ Hope it won't cost you much.

Tim: I hired a contractor to repair it. And the contractor did a very bad job. I need to buy some wax to wax the floor.

Greg: _____4_____ My wife and I usually wax the floor ourselves.

Tim: Is it very hard and complicated?

Greg: _____5_____. You just follow the instructions. It's simple.

Tim: Well, I'll try it anyway. My wife suggests that I should try to do it myself. Nice talking to you.

(　　) 1. (A) My blood pressure.   (B) Nothing special.

        (C) Everything is up now.   (D) Nothing at all.

(　　) 2. (A) how have you been?   (B) you really have good memory.

        (C) I just can't believe it.   (D) it has been quite a while.

(　　) 3. (A) Sorry to hear that.   (B) That sounds incredible.

        (C) Can you believe that?   (D) How much will that cost?

(　　) 4. (A) Do you know where to get it?

        (B) Are you going to do it yourself?

        (C) Maybe I can help you with that.

        (D) The wax will cost me a lot.

(　　) 5. (A) Yes, it's not that complicated.   (B) Yes, you are right.

        (C) No, it's not easy.   (D) No, it's easy.

Listening Activities

Sentence Dictation

Listen to the sentences on the tape carefully, and fill in the missing words in the blanks.

1. We called for a _____ to fix the problems of the _____.

2. _____ give complete _____ for building cabinets.

3. Follow the _____, you can put tile in bathrooms, _____ windows, and even enlarge a home.

4. There are guidebooks on wallpapering, _____, _____, and electrical wiring.

5. These small stores sell all kinds of _____ –from hammers and saws to _____ and wrenches.

6. Finishing a _____ repair or improvement gives them a great sense of _____.

7. The _____ of learning a new skill is the _____ of DIY.

8. Many homeowners hire _____ to do their _____ repairs.

9. There are _____ tapes that teach people how to _____ wooden floors, clean _____, and _____ houses.

10. A sense of _____ can be _____ from doing household _____.

Tell What They Are

Listen carefully and tell what their jobs are.

Name	Job
1. Peter	_____
2. James	_____
3. Tony	_____
4. Sandy	_____
5. Grace	_____
6. George	_____
7. Henry	_____
8. David	_____
9. Larry	_____
10. Bill	_____

Dialogue Comprehension

Listen to the dialogue on the tape carefully. According to what you hear, answer all the questions.

1. They hire _____ to do their _____.

2. They can _____.

3. They enjoy _____ and have a _____.

4. They go there to find _____ they need.

5. They need a few _____, good _____, and a little

_____.

Writing Activities

Sentence Completion

Use your own words to complete the following.

1. Experienced plumbers can fix problems with _____ at your house.

2. An electrician repairs problems with _____ at your house, too.

3. There are many _____ available that make _____ easy to do.

4. They _____ so much that they _____.

5. There are programs that _____.

6. In addition to _____ , larger stores also sell _____.

7. With a few necessary tools, you can become _____.

8. We can learn such things as _____ from DIY.

9. Carpenters can fix problems with _____.

10. Good instructions are _____ for _____ to

_____.

Composition

In 100 words write a short text to tell your friends how to make Chinese tea. Show the steps of making Chinese tea.

_____

_____

_____

_____

_____

_____

_____

_____

_____

_____

_____

_____

_____

_____

Acknowledgments

Body Painting

From *Body Language-Codes and Ciphers-Communicating by Signs, Writing and Numbers.* Published by Wayland (Publishers) Ltd. Reprinted by permission of the publisher.

Good Luck, Bad Luck

From *Project Achievement: Reading B.* (c) 1982 by Scholastic Inc. Reprinted by permission of Scholastic Inc.

Language in Clothes

From *Body Language-Codes and Ciphers-Communicating by Signs, Writing and Numbers.* Published by Wayland (Publishers) Ltd. Reprinted by permission of the publisher.

Animal Communication

From *Body Language-Codes and Ciphers-Communicating by Signs, Writing and Numbers.* Published by Wayland (Publishers) Ltd. Reprinted by permission of the publisher.

Take a Walk

From *Project Achievement: Reading D.* (c) 1984 by Scholastic Inc. Reprinted by permission of Scholastic Inc.

Are You an Eco-tourist?

From *Move Up* by Simon Greenall, published by Heinemann Publishers (Oxford) Ltd. (c) 1995. Reprinted by permission of Heinemann Educational Publishers, a division of Reed Educational & Professional Publishing Ltd.

Accepting Compliments

From *Communicator I* by MOLINSKY/BLISS, (c) 1994. Reprinted by permission of Prentice-Hall, Inc., Upper Saddle River, NJ.

Do-It-Yourself

From *Expressway 4*, 2nd ed. by Steven J. Molinsky and Bill Bliss, (c) 1997. Reprinted by permission of Prentice-Hall, Inc., Upper Saddle River, NJ.

一本最符合英語學習者需求的辭典!

三民 全球英漢辭典

莊信正、楊榮華主編

◎ 詞彙蒐羅詳盡,全書詞目超過93,000項。

◎ 釋義清晰明瞭,以樹枝狀的概念,將每個字彙分成「基本義」與「衍生義」,使讀者對字彙的理解更具整體概念。

◎ 以學習者的需要為出發點,將臺灣英語學習者最需要的語言資料詳實涵括在本書各項單元中。

◎ 新增「搭配用詞」一欄,列出詞語間的常用組合,增進你的語感,幫助你寫出、說出道地的英文。

讓你掌握英語的慣用搭配方式,學會道道地地的英語!

三民 新英漢辭典(增訂完美版)

◎ 收錄詞目增至67,500項(詞條增至46,000項)。

◎ 新增「搭配」欄,列出常用詞語間的組合關係,讓你掌握英語的慣用搭配,說出道地的英語。

◎ 附有精美插圖千餘幅,輔助詞義理解。

◎ 附錄包括詳盡的「英文文法總整理」、「發音要領解說」,提升學習效率。

一般辭典查不到的文化意涵,讓它來告訴你!

美國日常語辭典

◎ 描寫美國真實面貌,讓你不只學好美語,更進一步瞭解美國社會與文化!

◎ 廣泛蒐集美國人日常生活的語彙,是一本能伴你暢遊美國的最佳工具書!

◎ 從日常生活的角度出發,自日常用品、飲食文化、文學、藝術、到常見俚語,帶領你感受美語及其所代表的文化內涵,讓學習美語的過程不再只是背誦單字和強記文法句型的單調練習。

專為需要經常查閱最新詞彙的你設計!

三民 袖珍英漢辭典

◎收錄詞條高達58,000字,從最新的專業術語、時事用詞到日常生活所需詞彙全數網羅!

◎輕巧便利的口袋型設計,最適於外出攜帶!

自然英語系列

自然英語系列

你將會發現：學英語竟然可以這麼自自然然、輕輕鬆鬆！

自然英語會話

大西泰斗著／Paul C. McVay著

用生動、簡單易懂的筆調，針對口語的特殊動詞表現、日常生活的口頭禪等方面，解說生活英語精髓，使你的英語會話更接近以英語為母語的人，更流利、更自然。

英文自然學習法（一）

大西泰斗著／Paul C. McVay著

針對被動語態、時態、進行式與完成式、Wh-疑問句與關係詞等重點分析解說，讓你輕鬆掌握英文文法的竅門。

英文自然學習法（二）

大西泰斗著／Paul C. McVay著

打破死背介系詞意義和片語的方式，將介系詞的各種衍生用法連繫起來，讓你自然掌握介系詞的感覺和精神。

英文自然學習法（三）

大西泰斗著／Paul C. McVay著

運用「兔子和鴨子」的原理，解說PRESSURE的MUST、POWER的WILL、UP / DOWN / OUT / OFF等用法的基本感覺，以及所衍生出各式各樣精采豐富的意思，讓你簡單輕鬆活用英語！